Praise for *Sudde*

"What makes the novel so enthralling is the intimate humanity of its characters. Enrigue demystifies them using a rich, baroque naturalism, cut by flippancy and goofy jokes (all hail to translator Natasha Wimmer for relaxed perfection in every key). . . . *Sudden Death* resembles the arts it celebrates: selective, dramatized, all dark gaps and sensual glare, bending naturalism to some post-God purpose, like Caravaggio. Building a luxuriant picture that only ignites into meaning when angled a certain way, like the feather artists. Throughout this mercurial novel, playing fast and loose with facts lets richer truths about the world emerge." —*The Washington Post*

"Writing with his customary intensity about his favorite sport, David Foster Wallace described tennis as 'chess on the run, beautiful and infinitely dense.' In his droll and erudite new novel, *Sudden Death*, Álvaro Enrigue provides his own distinct take on that chess-on-the-run notion and elevates it to an even more exalted level. . . . [G]lorious . . . [H]is approach has both great entertainment value and intellectual appeal, especially as a corrective to a Eurocentric view of history. . . . *Sudden Death* is Mr. Enrigue's fifth novel, but only the first to be translated into English (and beautifully so by Natasha Wimmer, who has also deftly rendered the most challenging of Roberto Bolaño's work). . . . *Sudden Death* is a splendid introduction to Mr. Enrigue's varied body of work." —*The New York Times*

"Brain-spinning." —Marlon James, Booker Prize–winning author of *A Brief History of Seven Killings*

"[A] novel without boundaries." —*O, The Oprah Magazine*

"Mind-bending." —*The Wall Street Journal*

"Engrossing . . . rich with Latin and European history." —*The New Yorker*

"[A] bawdy, often profane, sprawling, ambitious book that is as engaging as it is challenging." —*Vogue*

"*Sudden Death* is the best kind of puzzle, its elements so esoteric and wildly funny that readers will race through the book, wondering how Álvaro Enrigue will be able to pull a novel out of such an astonishing ball of string. But Enrigue absolutely does; and with brilliance and clarity and emotional warmth all the more powerful for its surreptitiousness."
—Lauren Groff, *New York Times*–bestselling author of *Fates and Furies*

"Here is a novel that does full justice to the phrase 'cutting edge': In the manner of its protagonist, Caravaggio, *Sudden Death* is at once formally audacious and piercingly humane."

—Garth Risk Hallberg, *New York Times*–bestselling author of *City on Fire*

"[A] novel of revolution in the spatial and historical sense of the word. . . . And structurally, *Sudden Death* isn't normative: a short screenplay and the author's emails are interspersed with short entries from obscure sporting dictionaries and excerpts from humanist classics. Chapters are short, enticing, and written with a casual erudition that whispers to readers that, no matter the apparent surprises of the game, the author is in full control. Enrigue muses on the nature of the novel and his intentions in writing *Sudden Death* as easily as he holds a candle to the obscure maneuvers of the powerful. And he has a poet's ear, beautifully attended to by Natasha Wimmer's translation. . . . *Sudden Death* shows us that games are never merely games, because no game is played without consequences." —*Los Angeles Times*

"This novel by one of Mexico's most innovative authors is a triumph of narrative skill, humour, and lightly worn erudition." —*The Financial Times*

"By turns intellectual and earthy, Enrigue's fictionalized account of Renaissance Europe and sixteenth-century Mexico is the best kind of history lesson: erudite without being stuffy, an entertaining work that incorporates the Counter-Reformation, the Spanish conquest of the Aztec empire, art history, and even a grammar lesson on Spanish diminutives into one mesmerizing narrative." —*San Francisco Chronicle*

"At once erudite and phantasmagoric." —*The Millions*

"Brilliantly original. The best new novel I've read this year." —Salman Rushdie

"[A]n exhilarating, funny, and surprisingly sexy read. Enrigue turns historical figures into real, flesh-and-blood people." —BuzzFeed

"Inventive . . . The book bounces back and forth between the old world and the new, the past and the present, conquistadors and Mayans, and much more as it reimagines history as a sometimes brutal and sometimes hilarious tennis match." —*Thrillist*

"Like the tennis court, fiction can be both a constrained and a constraining space. . . . Enrigue teasingly suggests that the only debt a novel has is to its own internal coherence. . . . In less able hands, this could all feel a bit labored, but in *Sudden Death* the postmodernist flourishes are never gimmicks. They are suited to their subject, reflecting and revealing the games and tricks of empires and of the histories they construct to justify themselves."

—*Bookforum*

"*Sudden Death* is very, very funny and it is unfailingly brilliant and I have no idea how to describe it—another one of its rare virtues. I might say it is about tennis, or history, or art, or absurdity, but more accurate would be to say, simply, that it's essential reading."   —Rivka Galchen

"A story of history plunging forward and the world at a defining moment. Rackets are raised; the court looms large. Finally a tale that truly defies the bounds of the novel."   —Enrique Vila-Matas

"*Sudden Death* is a unique object—tropical and transatlantic; hypermodern and antiquarian—a specialized literary instrument designed to resist the deadly certainties of universal history. But don't let that confuse you. Sure, his method may be all playfulness and multiplicity, but Álvaro Enrigue is the most disabused novelist I know."

—Adam Thirlwell, author of *Lurid & Cute*

"A full-fledged writer."   —Mario Vargas Llosa

"[Enrigue] belongs to many literary traditions at once and shows a great mastery of them all. . . . His novel belongs to Max Planck's quantum universe rather than the relativistic universe of Albert Einstein: a world of coexisting fields in constant interaction and whose particles are created or destroyed in the same act."   —Carlos Fuentes

"In this wildly surreal novel—translated by Natasha Wimmer, who also translated Roberto Bolaño—the Mexican-born author imagines a sixteenth-century tennis match between the Italian painter Caravaggio and the Spanish poet Francisco de Quevedo played with a ball made from the hair of the beheaded Anne Boleyn. And then things really get strange."   —*Newsday*

"A rare example of an artful, comedic, deeply literary novel with the potential to become a fixture on bookshelves everywhere."   —*Flavorwire*

"Beautifully rendered . . . *Sudden Death* is one of the most engaging, audacious, and flat-out fun works of fiction I've read in a while."   —Vice.com

"Exuberantly intellectual . . . Enrigue transmutes the familiar, and shifts our awareness. *Sudden Death* is an original, transformative work."   —BBC.com

"The latest novel from Álvaro Enrigue defies any kind of easy description. . . . If you like your fiction both gripping and impossible to categorize, this may be your new obsession."   —*Vol. 1 Brooklyn*

"This rich novel will make the world come alive for you in completely new ways."   —*Bustle*

"Álvaro Enrigue's *Sudden Death* reads more like an intoxicating adventure than a novel—set around the world in the sixteenth century, *Sudden Death* presents familiar players (Galileo, Caravaggio, Anne Boleyn, Cortés, and more) like we've never seen them before. Spectacularly original, Enrigue's daring novel challenges everything readers think they know about European colonialism, history, art, and modernity."
     —BuzzFeed (Most Exciting Books Coming in 2016)

"Joyfully disorienting . . . Enrigue's ambitious tale bends in on itself and will reward readers who won't mind feeling like wanderers lost in the increasingly erudite corridors of Borges' library of Babel."   —*Booklist*

"*Sudden Death* reads like a playful novel written by a master with a wicked serve . . . not only does the reader get to brawl, drink, and love with Caravaggio, but Enrigue slides effortlessly between the tennis match and discourses that turn into philosophical art history. . . . The effect of these quick chapters is dazzling without being inaccessible."   —*Kirkus Reviews*

Sudden Death

ÁLVARO ENRIGUE

Translated by Natasha Wimmer

RIVERHEAD BOOKS

New York

RIVERHEAD BOOKS
An imprint of Penguin Random House LLC
375 Hudson Street
New York, New York 10014

First published in Spain in 2013 by Anagrama, as *Muerte súbita*
Copyright © 2013 by Álvaro Enrigue
English translation copyright © 2016 by Natasha Wimmer

First Riverhead hardcover edition: February 2016
First Riverhead trade paperback edition: February 2017
Riverhead hardcover ISBN: 9781594633461
Riverhead trade paperback ISBN: 9780735213449

Printed in the United States of America
3   5   7   9   10   8   6   4

BOOK DESIGN BY NICOLE LAROCHE

For La Flaca Luiselli

For the three Garcías: Maia, Miqui, Dy

For Hernán Sánchez de Pinillos

The oldest written record of the word *tennis* makes no mention of athletic shoes; rather, it refers solely to the sport from which they take their name, a sport that—along with fencing, its near kin—was one of the first to require a special kind of footwear.

In 1451, Edmund Lacey, Bishop of Exeter, defined the game with the same suppressed rage with which my mother referred to the falling-apart Converse I wore as a kid: *ad ludum pile vulgariter nuncupatum Tenys*. In Lacey's edict, the word *tenys*—in the vernacular—is linked to phrases with the acid whiff of court cases: *prophanis colloquiis et iuramentis, vanis et sepissime periuriis illicitis, sepius rixas*.

At the collegiate church of Ottery St. Mary, under Lacey's rule, a group of novices had been using the roofed gallery of the cloister to play matches against townies. In those days, tennis was much rougher and noisier than it is today: some were attackers, others defenders; there were no nets or lines; and points were won tooth and nail, by slamming the ball into an opening called a dedans. Since it was a sport invented by Mediterranean monks, it had redemptive overtones: angels on one side, demons on the other. It was a matter of death and the afterlife, the ball as allegory of the soul flitting between good and evil, scheming to get into heaven, Lucifer's messengers waylaying it. The soul rent asunder, just like my tennis shoes.

The prickly Baroque painter Michelangelo Merisi da Caravaggio, a great lover of the game, spent his last years in exile for having run an opponent through with his sword on a tennis court. Today, the Roman street where the crime was committed is called Via di Pallacorda—"street of the ball and net"—in memory of the incident. Caravaggio was sentenced to death by beheading in Rome and spent years living as a fugitive, from Naples to Sicily to the island of Malta. Between commissions, he painted terrifying scenes of beheadings in which he served as his own model for the severed heads. He sent the paintings to the pope or his agents as symbolic tribute, in the hope of being pardoned. At the age of thirty-eight, Caravaggio was at last granted a reprieve, and he was on his way back to Rome when he was stabbed on the Tuscan beach of Porto Ercole, by an assassin sent by the Knights of Malta. Though he was a master of the sword and dagger, just as he was of the brush and racket, syphilitic delirium and lead poisoning left him unable to defend himself. *Sepius rixas.*

A few years ago I attended one of the three hundred thousand book fairs held every week across the Spanish-speaking world. A local literary critic found me so intolerable that he decided to launch a jeremiad against me. Since he didn't have the time or energy to read a whole book and take it apart, he wrote on his blog: "How dare he appear in public wearing tennis shoes like that?" *Vanis et sepissime periuriis illicitis!*

It's no surprise that anyone possessing a modicum of authority should agitate against tennis, or tennis shoes. I myself often issue complaints, like bad checks, about my teenage son's Adidas. We cling to our tennis shoes until wearing them on a rainy day is agony. Anyone in a position of power hates them, impervious as they are to their agendas.

When this book first appeared, in Spanish, a Canadian writer and very dear friend of mine told his father, who was wildly excited because he felt that fiction writing had yet to pay real tennis its due in the form of a novel. He doesn't speak Spanish, but he is perfectly fluent in French and Italian, which makes him capable enough of reading a book written in my mother tongue, so he had a copy sent to him from Spain and read it with the help of a dictionary. I can't imagine a greater honor for a writer, though I'm not sure my friend's father liked the book. In an attempt to save me from my own imagination, he wrote me a six-page letter pointing out all the physical impossibilities and imaginary rules I had come up with to be able to say whatever this book says. The letter proves that the true art is reading, not writing, and it is a beautiful testament of loyalty: a friend of his son is a friend of his. Commenting on some sexual incidents described in the novel, he noted: "Now I know why you and my son are friends." This is a statement of complicity. It tells me that if we knew each other, he would forgive my defects just as he does his son's. And his letter is full of authority. Not the kind that comes with age or rank, since I'm well past forty and a father myself, but the kind that comes with firsthand knowledge. My characters are playing *pallacorda*, a game whose rules are unknown, but physical memory, a sense of how the real tennis racket feels in the hand and how a real tennis ball bounces, made my friend's father file a claim in the name of all realism. But the only real things in a novel are the sequences of letters, words, and sentences that make it up, and the paper on which they're printed. What they produce in a reader's head are private and unique landscapes of objects in motion that have only one thing in common: they don't exist. A game that is played in a novel has everything to do with that novel and nothing to do with reality. And even so, we tend to claim—as my friend's father did—that certain things are to be believed and others not in this or that book. As if a ball dropped by a character could roll out of a book onto the floor, run up against our tennis shoes, and stop.

In the opening scene of the British Renaissance comedy *Eastward Ho*, an apprentice called Quicksilver makes his appearance wrapped in a cloak and wearing pumps—slippers with thick woolen soles that are the earliest forerunners of our tennis shoes. His master, troubled by what he sees as a sign that the young man is about to fall into the company of ruffians, gamblers, and assassins, lifts the apprentice's cloak. From his belt hang a sword and a tennis racket. Another in a line of authority figures—mothers, fathers, critics, bishops, bosses—alerted to someone's essential flaws by his athletic shoes.

When leather footwear begins to look shabby, we take it to the cobbler to give it the sad newness of faces worked over by a plastic surgeon. Tennis shoes are one of a kind: there is no fixing them. What value they have derives from the scars left by our missteps. My first pair of Converse met a sudden death. One day I came home from school and my mother had thrown them away.

It's no coincidence that when speaking of someone's death in Mexico we say he "hung up his tennis shoes," that he "went out tennis shoes first." We are who we are, unfixable, fucked. We wear tennis shoes. We fly from good to evil, from happiness to responsibility, from jealousy to sex. Souls batted back and forth across the court. This is the serve.

First Set,
First Game

◆——•——◆

He felt the leather of the ball between the thumb, index, and middle fingers of his left hand. Once, twice, three times he bounced the ball on the pavement, spinning the racket handle in the grip of his right hand. For a moment he gauged the space of the court; his hangover made the midday sun seem unbearably bright. He took a deep breath: the tennis match that was about to begin was a contest of life and death.

Wiping the beads of sweat from his forehead, he rolled the ball again in the fingers of his left hand. It was a strange ball: very worn and much handled, a little smaller than usual, solid in a way that was recognizably French; it had a more hectic bounce than the balls filled with air that he was used to playing with in Spain. He glanced down and with his toe scraped the stripe of lime that marked the end of his side of the court. He would come down on his short leg just behind the line: this was the surprise factor that made him invincible with a sword, and perhaps—why not?—with a racket too.

He heard laughter from his opponent, who was waiting for the serve on the other side of the cord strung between them. One of the degenerates accompanying him had muttered something in Italian. At least one of them was familiar: a man with a jutting nose, red beard, and sad eyes—the model for the tax-collector saint in *The Calling of Saint Matthew*, proud recent acquisition of the church of San Luigi dei Francesi. Tossing the ball in the air, he shouted *Tenez!* and felt the catgut strings tighten as he lit into it with all his soul.

His opponent's eyes followed the ball as it flew toward the gallery roof. It struck at one of the corners. The Spaniard smiled: his first serve was lethal, untouchable. The Lombard had rested too easy, so sure was he that a lame man could be no match for him. In the quick, shrill voice with which Castilians pierce walls and minds, the poet remarked: Better a cripple than a bugger. On the other side of the court, no one laughed at his joke. But from his spot in the roofed gallery, the duke watched with the sly smile of a great rake.

In time, the duke, the poet's linesman, would become the Spanish statesman his title gave him the right to be, but by the autumn of 1599 he had done nothing but punish his body, sully the family name, worry his wife sick, and drive the king's counselors to distraction. He was a stout, brash man. He had a round face, an almost comically pointy nose, grapefruit-seed eyes that gave him a mocking aspect even when he was in earnest, short curly hair, and an unconvincing beard that made him look more of a fool than he was. He was watching the match in the same scornful, sardonic way he did everything, sitting in the arcade under the wooden roof on which the ball had to bounce for a serve to be considered good.

The Lombard took the center of the court behind the baseline. He waited in a crouch for the bounce of the Spaniard's serve. The gang of layabouts with him preserved a respectful silence this time. The poet served again, and again he won the point. He had put the ball almost on his own side of the roof, so that it fell nearly dead for his opponent. The duke called out the score: Thirty–love, though what he said was "lof." The Italians understood perfectly.

Gaining confidence, the Spaniard dried the palm of his right hand on his breeches. He turned the ball in his left. He was sweating enough to give it backspin without needing to spit on it. It wasn't the heat but the fever that afflicts those who have yet to recover from too much drink, landing them in a purgatory of shivers. He rolled his head from side to side, closed his eyes, and wiped his mouth with his sleeve. He squeezed the ball. It wasn't a normal ball; there was something irregular about it, as if it were more talisman than ball. This, it occurred to him, was why his serves were unstoppable. When he took his turn on the receiving side and the ball returned to the hands of its owner, he would have to take heed.

He gripped the racket and tossed the ball into the air. *Tenez!* He hit it so hard that for the fraction of a second before his lame leg came down again, the earth seemed to turn more slowly. The ball bounced capriciously on the roof of the gallery. The Lombard stretched for it. The Spaniard tried to kill the return dead but didn't manage it. The point continued: luckily for him, the ball struck one of the posts, and he was able to snag it on the bounce, driving it to the back of the court. It was a good save, but the maneuver took too long, and surprise was the only option he had for countering his opponent's experience on the court. The Lombard found it simple to fling himself backward and hit a drive that the poet had no chance of returning.

Thirty–fifteen, cried the duke. The only responsible member of the Lombard's entourage was his linesman—a silent and prematurely aged professor of mathematics. He walked onto the court to mark a chalk cross on the spot where the ball had bounced. Before he made the mark he turned to look at the Spaniard's second. The duke shrugged in a show of indifference, agreeing that the cross was well-placed.

The poet didn't return immediately to position. While the professor took his time with the marking, he went over to the gallery. He's good, the duke said when the poet was near; you couldn't hit a ball like that on your best day. The poet filled his cheeks with air and blew it out with a snort. I can't lose, he said. You can't lose, confirmed the duke.

The next point was long and hard-fought. The Spaniard had his back to the wall, returning balls as if besieged by an army. Move in, move in, the duke cried every so often, but each time the poet managed to advance a little, his attacker pushed him back. At a desperate moment, he had to curb a drive by turning his back on his opponent—a showy play, but not very practical. The Lombard got to the ball close in and drilled the wall again. The ball struck very near the dedans—if it had gone in, the artist would automatically have won the game. Thirty all, cried the duke. *Parità*, the professor confirmed. The poet hit a serve that struck the edge of the gallery. Inside and unreachable. Forty–thirty, cried the duke. The mathematician nodded serenely.

The next point was contested with more cunning than strength: the poet didn't let himself be trapped, and he was finally able to force the artist to play a corner. On the first short ball he eliminated him. Game, called the duke. *Caccia per Spagna,* called the professor.

Rule

❖

Tennis. Game of a likeness to handball. One player defends and the other attacks, then vice versa. If there is a tie, a chase will decide the defender and the attacker in the third round, which is called sudden death. On the serve, the ball must strike a slant roof along one side of the court, from which it drops and is returned. Tennis is also called *pala*, after the racket with which the game is played, which is made entirely of wood with a little net of tight-strung gut in the center. It is gripped by the handle and with it the ball is struck with violence and force. Tennis is scored by points, but he who hits the dedans wins a round and he who wins three straight rounds or four rounds divided wins the match.

Diccionario de autoridades, Madrid, 1726

Beheading

◆—•—◆

Jean Rombaud had the worst of all possible tasks on the morning of May 19, 1536: severing with a single blow the head of Anne Boleyn, Marquess of Pembroke and Queen of England, a young woman so beautiful she had turned the Strait of Dover into a veritable Atlantic. The notorious Thomas Cromwell, chief minister to Henry VIII, had brought Rombaud over from France for this express purpose. In a curt missive, Cromwell asked that he bring his sword—a piece of miraculously fine craftsmanship, forged of Toledo steel—because he would be performing a delicate execution.

Rombaud was neither beloved nor indispensable. Beautiful and immoral, he drifted coldly in the tight circle of very specialized workers who thrived in the Renaissance courts under the blind eye of ambassadors, ministers, and secretaries. His reserve, striking looks, and lack of scruples made him a natural for certain kinds of tasks known to all and spoken of by none, the dark operations that have always been unavoidable in the conduct of politics. He dressed with surprising good taste for someone with the job of killer angel: he wore expensive rings, breeches lavishly trimmed with brocade, and royal-blue velvet shirts unsuited to a bastard, which he was in every sense of the word. Cheap gemstones were braided with gypsy panache into his gold-streaked chestnut hair, the gems filched from mistresses conquered with the various weapons over which God had granted him mastery. There was no knowing whether he was silent because he was clever or because he was a fool: his deep blue eyes, which turned down a little at the corners, never expressed compassion, but they never expressed any kind of animosity either. Also, Rombaud was French: for him, killing a queen of England was less sin than duty. Cromwell had called him to London because he believed this last quality made him a particularly hygienic choice for the job.

It wasn't King Henry who had arranged for his wife's death by Toledo sword rather than by the lowly blow of the ax that separated her brother's head from his neck on the accusation he had slept with the queen, a sin that earned him the record sum of three death sentences: for lèse-majesté, for adultery, and for degeneracy. No one—not even the notorious Thomas Cromwell—could bear for such a neck as hers to be hacked by the coarse blade of an ax.

On the morning of May 19, 1536, Anne Boleyn attended mass and made her confession. Before she was turned over to the constable of the Tower so her body could be cleaved apart, she asked that her ladies-in-waiting alone be given the privilege of cropping her heavy red braids and shaving her head. Most of the surviving portraits, including the sole copy of the only one reportedly painted from life—now part of Hever Castle's Tudor portrait collection—depict her as the owner of crimped and significant locks.

It seems that the royal bedchamber had a dampening effect on King Henry's libido, such a champion was he in extramarital affairs—and such an underperformer in his royal reproductive duties. No one knew this better than the marquess of Pembroke, who had managed to conceive by him after a single day in the country, while he was still married to his previous queen. They'd had a daughter as lovely as the marquess herself, for whom the monarch professed the thunderous affection associated with homicidal types. So Anne Boleyn approached the scaffold conscious of the statistical odds that her daughter, Elizabeth, would reach the throne, as indeed she ultimately did. Boleyn delivered herself into martyrdom with a show of calculated cheer. Among her last words, pronounced before the witnesses to her death, were: "I pray God save the King, and send him long to reign over you, for a gentler nor a more merciful prince was there never."

What is it about nudity, in theory the great equalizer, that excites us? In their naked state, only monsters should turn us on, and yet it's the very sameness of our nakedness that we find arousing. The ladies who accompanied Boleyn in her trials had pulled back the collar of her gown to reveal her neck before escorting her to the scaffold. They had also removed her necklaces. They didn't feel that the removal of her veil and tresses marred her beauty in the least: she was just as lovely with a shorn head as she was with hair.

The bluish gleam of her neck quivering in anticipation of the blow triggered an emotional response in Rombaud. According to one witness, the mercenary was kind enough to make an effort to surprise the lady lying there bare from her shoulder blades to the crown of her head. With his sword raised high and ready to come down upon the queen's neck, he asked carelessly: Has anyone seen my sword? The woman twitched her shoulders, perhaps relieved that some chance occurrence might spare her. She closed her eyes. Vertebrae, cartilage, the spongy tissue of trachea and pharynx: the sound of their parting was like the elegant pop of a cork liberated from a bottle of wine.

Jean Rombaud refused the bag of silver coins that Thomas Cromwell offered him when the job was done. Addressing the whole gathering, but looking into the eyes of the man who had schemed until he unseated the queen, he said that he had agreed to do what he had done to spare a lady the vile fate of dying under an executioner's blade. He made a sideways bow to the ministers and clergymen who had witnessed the beheading, and he returned straight to Dover at full gallop. Earlier that morning, the lord high constable had packed the categorical braids of the queen of England in his saddlebags.

Rombaud was an avid tennis player, and this seemed sufficient payment: the hair of those executed on the scaffold had special properties that caused it to trade at stratospheric prices among ball makers in Paris. A woman's hair was worth more, red hair more still, and a reigning queen's would command an unimaginable price.

Anne Boleyn's braids produced a total of four balls, which were by far the most luxurious sporting equipment of the Renaissance.

On the Nobility
of the Game
# of Tennis

First we shall see how the game of tennis has been ordered to excellent and rational ends, which is how all worthy and valuable art should be, in imitation of nature, which does nothing without great mastery. Note, for example, how the ancient and wise inventors of this game, considering that it inflames and impassions even the palest and weakest youth, contrived it in such a fashion that the player is never hurt. As will subsequently be explained, the ball is not hit while it is in the air, but rather after it has bounced on the ground, making it impossible for the receiving player to be injured. Similarly, the receiving player waits for the bounce to learn whether the point he intends to make is valid. If he wants the advantage, he is obliged to display the requisite decency and allow the other player equal time to recover.

ANTONIO SCAINO, *Treatise on the Game of the Ball*,
Venice, 1555

First Set, Second Game

———◆•◆———

Before the start of the second game, the Spaniard approached his linesman. He's a strong player and he knows the court, said the duke; you won the first game because he didn't expect anything of you. I'm younger, replied the poet; I can match him for strength. But you have a lame leg. The surprise factor, and I'll play twice as hard; should I move in? He'll break you with those drives of his. I'll bring him short. Then you'd be putting everything in the hands of fate; better to wear him down, it's clear he won't last; take it point by point: backward, forward, play the corners. The poet snorted and wiped the sweat from his forehead, looking down with his hands on his hips, as if waiting for clearer instructions. If he hadn't been in the grips of a hangover, the prospect of such a match might've seemed less insurmountable. It'll be close, he said. Concession is the other option, said the duke, but the duel was your idea. The poet stared at the ground: We could turn to swords, finish up quick. The duke shook his head: Not another scandal, and he's a wild man with the blade. The poet grunted: I haven't lost yet. Precisely. Very well, I'll take it point by point. Before he returned to the court, he said: Have you noticed they don't speak to each other? Who? He and his second. The duke didn't see that it mattered: What of it? Last night they didn't speak either, they don't even seem to be friends, look at them. His opponent hadn't gone near the gallery. The mathematician languished, gazing at the specks of dust floating in the air.

The scrutiny of both men turned naturally on the artist, the poet's rival. The seriousness of his manner did nothing to lighten their mood. He was less cocksure than before, but even more determined. Now, rather than a matter of life or death, it was a matter of victory or defeat—a much more complex affair, and harder to bear because the loser of a duel by sword isn't obliged to live with the consequences.

The poet continued to study his opponent. He was a pallid man, with unruly jet-black hair sticking up all over his head. He had bushy eyebrows and a thick, untidy beard circling a mouth dark red like a cunt. The poet squinted to see him better. He was strong, sturdy as a soldier despite his generally unwholesome air: a member of the Neapolitan corps returned from the dead to play a last game of tennis in order to prove who-knowswhat to the living. Does he always look so unwell, or is it just the hangover, he asked the duke. Who? The painter. I don't know, I was watching his linesman. The mathematician, sitting on his own in the gallery, was scanning the court, scrutinizing it with disturbing intensity. His lips moved. What is there to see? He's a professor. So? He's no fool, the whoreson is counting something. The poet hawked up phlegm and shrugged. He spat: Let's go.

He picked up the ball and called: *Tenez?* The monster stared at him, as if from the far bank of the river of the dead, and nodded, unsmiling. He blew at the hair falling over his left eye. His forehead was beaded not with sweat but with oil. From the line of service, the Spaniard noted that his opponent and the professor were in fact communicating: the linesman produced sequences of numbers with his fingers, sometimes pointing up, sometimes down, sometimes toward his own body. The poet indicated this to his linesman, pointing his racket at the Italians. The duke clenched his jaw, uneasy. The poet bounced the ball on the line, tossed it in the air: *Tenez!*

It was a mediocre serve and the return was savage. The artist met the ball in the air and sent it with brute strength straight into the poet's face. Though he tried to protect himself, he took the blow between neck and cheek. *Quindici–amore*, cried the professor clinically, in the harsh voice of a market vendor but without a hint of irony.

The poet ducked his head, stung by the blow. He looked up carefully, for fear of swooning, and rubbed his jaw, seeking out his opponent in search of an explanation: he had never seen anything like this. The artist folded his hands over the handle of his racket, as if in prayer. It was a gesture of apology, an acknowledgment of a lack of sportsmanship. The duke raised the skin on his face that occupied the place where anyone else would have eyebrows. The poet pressed thumb and forefinger to his temples, then picked up the ball and, without further ado, returned to the line of service. The duke could tell his player was shaken by the way he readied himself for the new serve: he was taking deep breaths. He noticed, too, that he spat on the ball with perhaps less discretion than might be advised in a game like this. No one said anything.

Tenez! He put the ball on the edge of the roof, nearly straight above the cord. The saliva made it bounce queerly. The Lombard didn't give chase, though he plainly could have reached it. He waited for the ball to stop rolling, picked it up, and dried it on his breeches before returning it, signaling that the Spaniard had cheated, though not protesting. The gesture was effective: it was one thing to break the rules of chivalry in an outburst of manly rage, and another to cheat furtively, like a nun. The poet felt disgust at himself. The duke didn't call the point. Do over, he cried.

The poet bounced the ball on the line, tossed it in the air. *Tenez!* The artist waited for it to drop from the roof and with 360 degrees of force, he pounded it with his racket as if it were a nail in Christ's wrist. The ball flew straight at the poet's face again, but this time he took it in the crown, managing to duck a little. *Trenta–amore,* called the professor.

The Spaniard got up with tears in his eyes, his head bent. When he picked up the ball he felt dizzy. He kneeled and rubbed his scalp. He couldn't even glance at the other side of the court: a smile from any of the louts in his opponent's entourage and he would go for his sword. What is this, he asked the duke in a tight voice as he got up. You're winning the game, *macho*; onward. What do I do? Nothing. Keep serving and victory will be your revenge.

The poet picked up the ball reluctantly; he was not at all convinced by his boss's strategy. There were less painful ways of winning a game. Just keep serving, the duke insisted.

Tenez! The ball dropped on the artist's side like a gift: it had bounced twice on the roof of the gallery and fallen in the middle of the court, floating like a feather. The poet felt the return when it hammered like a stone straight into his balls. He never even saw it. He fell solidly to the ground like a quarry block. From a world in ruins, he heard the mathematician crying: *Amore, amore, amore, amore; vittoria rabbiosa per lo spagnolo.*

Even the duke was doubled over, quaking with laughter, when the poet raised his head. Not to mention his opponent, Saint Matthew, the mathematician, and all the other wastrels, who were hugging their stomachs and wiping away tears of mirth.

Soul

❯━━━━◆•━━━━❮

In the year 1767, the French encyclopaedist François Alexandre de Garsault, author of various manuals for the fabrication of luxury goods such as wigs, underclothing, and sporting equipment—"trivial arts," as he himself noted in the second edition of his *Art du paumier-racquetier*—still distinguished between two kinds of tennis balls: proper balls, made of batting and thread and covered with stitched white cloth, and *éteufs*, or skin balls—which in Spanish were called *pellas* well into the seventeenth century—made of lumps of lard, flour, and hair.

The *éteufs*, covered with calfskin and cross-stitched, resembled our baseballs, with the suture exposed. While the cloth balls were used only on inside courts of hardwood or tile, and tended to come apart after three or four matches, the skin balls could be used for years without any loss of nimbleness or violence: they were intended to bounce on the tiles and roofs of cloisters and the uneven clay of town squares, where tennis was played for money.

In the third decade of the twentieth century, the team that restored the roof of the main hall in the Palace of Westminster found two balls in the beams that date indisputably from the sixteenth century. They were intact. A genetic analysis of the hair from which they were made showed no evidence of a connection with any branch of the Boleyn family. No great surprise: many terrible things may be said about Henry VIII, but not that he had bad taste. Certainly, then, he never bought or accepted as a gift any of the balls of which he might—curiously enough—be called the widower.

François Alexandre de Garsault's Enlightenment manual contains no instructions for making balls out of human hair. Perhaps he was unaware that during the Renaissance and Baroque periods the material was common currency in the outdoor courts where tennis was a betting sport. Nor does it seem that Garsault, practical man and earnest educator, was a great reader of literature: in *Much Ado About Nothing*, the inveterate bachelor Benedick has so much facial hair that, according to Shakespeare, his beard has filled many a tennis ball.

From the study of the balls found in the rafters of Westminster Hall, as well as certain clues that come to light when one combs through Antonio Scaino's rambling *Trattato del giuoco della palla* (1555), it may be deduced that the core of the *pella* was identical to that of the proper salon balls: a base of batting kneaded with paste. The base of the salon ball was then wrapped in strips of linen and thread and tapped into shape with a putty knife. Once calibrated, the ball was tied with a string that divided it into nine sections through its upper pole. Then the ball was spun 45 degrees and another nine sections were traced through a second pole. And again, until there were nine poles with nine equators. Each ball a world, a planet dotted with eighty-one ribbons of thread. Finally, the little orb—believed by the ancients to represent the human soul—was covered in cloth and whitewashed.

The *pella* was fabricated according to a similar procedure, but in more sordid and often clandestine settings: there was something grisly about making balls with human hair, and not everyone was willing to produce an object that took its life from the only part of a dead body that doesn't rot. In place of the strips of linen, locks of hair were bound around the core and stuck down with lard and flour. It was a lighter ball, less smooth; it bounced like a thing possessed.

Probably because of its soul of human matter, during the Renaissance and Baroque periods the *pella* was associated in Catholic Europe and Conquest-era America with satanic pursuits.

The Boleyn Balls

———— • ————

Scarcely had Jean Rombaud disembarked at Franciscopolis—such was the ridiculous name of the port of Le Havre until the death of King Francis I—before he began to spread the rumor that he was in possession of the darksome braids of Anne Boleyn and that he would make tennis balls with them that would at last gain him entry to the closed courts, where the nobility sweated through one shirt per game, five per set, and fifteen per match. He had always felt that his fresh-washed lion's mane gave him the right to hardwood and tile: to play for sport rather than money.

By the time the ball maker delivered the four most bewitching balls in the history of Europe, a multitude of buyers had approached Rombaud, offering prices out of all proportion to the size of his treasure: one hundred cows, a villa in Provence, two African slaves, six horses. He declined all invitations to discuss, except that of Philippe de Chabot, minister to the king.

To this negotiation he brought only the fourth ball, a bit smaller and more tightly wound than the others, which from the start he had decided to keep for himself as an amulet. He brought it wrapped in a silk cloth, deep in his purse, which for greater security he had sewn into the lining of his cloak.

Chabot received him in his bedchamber as he was being dressed. It wasn't the first time they had met. Jean Rombaud had prepared a brief discourse that didn't skimp on the honeyed rhetoric of a sloe-eyed villain, and which progressed from pleading to blackmail. The minister didn't ask him to sit, nor did he allow him to make his case. He didn't even turn to look at him, focused as he was on his servants swaddling him in linens and velvets. What do you want for the balls of the heretic pig, he asked, staring intently at the point of his shoe. I've brought one with me as a sample, replied Rombaud, drawing it clumsily from his cloak. The minister brushed a wisp of cloth from his knee, ignoring the object that the executioner held out to him reverently from across the room. We are assured, said Chabot without turning to look at the ball, that they are authentic, because the ambassador of the king of Spain tried to secure the braids for his own conjurations and flew into a rage when he learned that the trophy was on its way to France. I want neither money nor possessions, said Rombaud. The minister lifted his palms in a gesture conveying both interrogation and exasperation. I want a modest title and a position in the royal court as master of fencing and tennis. It can be arranged, but first bring me the balls. I want the king himself to grant me both things; I want it to be in the presence of witnesses and I want him to look me in the eye. The minister glanced at him for the first time, raising his eyebrows in ironic puzzlement. The king is a little busy taking back Savoy, he said, but we'll call for you when he comes through Paris; the balls will make a nice treat for him;

bring them with you the day my messenger commands you to appear at the Louvre.

Seventy-three days later, Jean Rombaud was received by King Francis I in the Salon Bleu, which was crammed with members of the court, petitioners, and financiers. The future fencing and tennis master was wearing a pompous fitted costume that he'd had made for the occasion. For once in his life he was rid of his intolerable three-day beard, and he had combed his bejeweled hair into a tail that he thought was elegant—and in its grave-digger way, it was, though possibly too Spanish for the salons of the king of France.

He didn't have to wait long in courtyards or antechambers: the king sent for him shortly after he presented himself, and showed a scarcely regal impatience to see the Bolcyn balls. Jean Rombaud wasn't allowed to deliver the lengthy address that he had prepared for this day either. Queen Eleanor approached to witness the great moment, trailing a train of ermine among the filthy boots of her husband's men. Francis I's eyes nearly glowed when he opened the carved wooden box that the mercenary had spent a fortune to have made—on credit, of course—and which had seemed magnificent at the inn where he lived but in the palace now looked small and paltry.

The king took one of the balls, weighed it with the calculation of a seasoned tennis player, squeezed it, and turned it in his hand. He pretended to toss it in the air and hit a serve with an imaginary racket. He felt the ball again, then discomfited his wife by putting his nose to it and inhaling deeply, revealing the urge—however remote—to lose himself in the braids that had been the downfall of King Henry and whose spell had snatched

England from the pope. Looking at Rombaud, he said at last: They say she was beautiful, yes? Even with a shorn head, Your Majesty, were the only words the poor man was able to speak to his king. Francis tossed the ball into the air and caught it gracefully. He looked out over the salon, cleared his throat as if to request the attention he always had, and said: The new fencing master is rather more handsome than I'd been told; he'll teach tennis at the court, too, so watch your daughters. The breath of polite laughter moved like a wave through the Salon Bleu. We grant him his request, said the king. He looked Rombaud in the eye: With privileges for life; we have spoken.

"In a New World and Land"

—•—

The fourth of October, 1599, was a sunny day in Rome. There's no evidence that Francisco de Quevedo was in the city on that particular day, but nor is there evidence that he was anywhere else. It is a fact that he did not occupy chair 58 in the solemn ceremony for the awarding of bachelor of arts degrees at the University of Alcalá de Henares, outside Madrid, where he certainly ought to have been.

The most often repeated theory regarding Quevedo's absence from his own graduation assumes that he was fleeing after a never-resolved murder—probably committed in Madrid—in which he played a part, along with his friend and protector Pedro Téllez Girón, Duke of Osuna and Marquis of Peñafiel.

Quevedo had met Girón many years earlier, when Francisco was a boy and Pedro a very young diplomat's apprentice in the service of the duke of Feria. Both were members of the extravagant delegation headed by the infanta Isabel Clara Eugenia, sent to the Estates-General of France to petition for the Crown of France. No crossing of the Pyrenees could have been more ridiculous, no convoy of high and low nobility more grotesque.

The man charged with presenting the infanta's impossible

candidacy was the duke of Feria. Pedro Téllez Girón—at the time only the marquis of Peñafiel, because his lackluster father was still alive—figured as his secretary. Francisco de Quevedo, aged eight, had come along because children traveled with their parents and he was the son of a lady-in-waiting to the infanta, present on the expedition. Quevedo's sister was there too; she was a child attendant, something like a lapdog.

What a crossing: carts bulging with items of a luxury smothering enough to enable the infanta to feel at home in any inn; carriages crammed with ladies in towering coiffures trailing lineages so lengthy that they spilled out the windows; the men ahead and on horseback, in breastplates trimmed with American gold as if to remind Paris that the world belonged to them, though Philip hadn't been as good as his father, Charles, at holding on to it; the children, and there must have been many, shoehorned in between chests and throwing clods and slabs of dirt at one another amid much hilarity. The purpose of this whole circus was to demand that the Estates-General crown Isabel Clara Eugenia, a thing that simply could not happen. France hadn't been governed by a woman since Salic law was adopted in 1316. Not to mention that the infanta was Spanish, left-handed, fat, a bit slow, chewed her fingernails, and picked her nose and ate it.

The list of personages who made the trip is preserved in the archives of the National Library of Spain, and Quevedo and Girón's names appear on it. There is also a travel log. In the diary of the secretary to the duke of Feria's mother, an entry made in Gerona dated June 27 laments that the delegation's delays and the inability of the poor infanta to command respect were turning the convoy into a carnival. The secretary writes: "Girón, never in earnest, goes about everywhere with a little maggot who calls Her Majesty 'La Elefanta.'" Who else could it be?

Girón and Quevedo met again many years later in Alcalá de Henares. Pedro Téllez Girón—by now duke of Osuna, a grandee of Spain—was, like his friend, a man of ready tongue and insatiable urges; a drunk and a brawler from first to last. A man who knew how to get himself into trouble—and out of it.

In the autumn of 1599 he was dogged by three trials. The first was a result of keeping company with the actress Jerónima de Salcedo, whom he had set up in his house in Alejos with her father and husband. Osuna got only a minor reprimand, but the actress and her family were sentenced to flogging, feathering, and parading, she for being a kept woman, her father for being a pimp, and her husband for being a cuckold.

Another trial, thornier this time, involved an uncle of Osuna's—a bastard son but an influential man—who had been his tutor. Juan de Ribera, Viceroy of Valencia, had accused this uncle of murdering his own wife and replacing her in the nuptial bed with a young page, with whom he apparently did the nefarious deed with scandalous enthusiasm and frequency.

Osuna's uncle and the page were garroted in the plaza and their bodies burned. Though it seemed that all Valencia could testify to their amours, Pedro Téllez Girón stood in his tutor's defense until the end and escaped unscathed, though he was sentenced to house arrest—where he must not have had such a bad time, because the actress and her family were still awaiting the conclusion of their own trial.

The third trial must have been by far the worst, because not a single official record is left of the crime he committed with another scoundrel, who might have been Quevedo. During this trial Osuna was jailed in Arévalo Prison and then locked up in his house in Osuna under the strict watch of four bailiffs. Historians and assorted amateurs have put two and two together and surmised that the sin for which Girón ended up in Arévalo was the murder of one or more soldiers in a dispute over a racket game.

In his *Account of Occurrences in the Court of Spain*, the historian Luis Cabrera de Córdoba reports that on August 6, 1599, while under house arrest, Osuna asked for leave to go to Madrid to kiss the king's hand, and, "having been granted it, he used it to go to Seville, and even—it is said—to Naples, to indulge his urges." It's more than likely that he brought along his comrade in revelry, who was also under house arrest at the time.

In Seville, Quevedo—his position vastly more precarious than Osuna's—must have tried to convince him that they should go to New Spain, like the narrator of *El Buscón*, an autobiographical novel he wrote soon afterward (though he never acknowledged authorship). "Seeing that this matter was of long duration," says his protagonist, "and that ill fortune pursued me ever more adamantly, I determined to remove myself to the Indies, not because I had learned my lesson—I am not so levelheaded—but out of weariness, as an inveterate sinner, in hopes that in a new world and land, my luck would improve."

It's very likely that, once in Seville, they did travel on to the south of Italy—which was within the comfortable embrace of empire yet not within easy reach of the bailiffs of Philip III. At the time, the viceroy of Naples and the Two Sicilies was the duke of Lerma, a close relative of Osuna's and protector of Quevedo's family. In the end—and this does show up in a number of documents—it was the wife of the viceroy of Naples, the duchess of Lerma, who obtained the royal pardon for the young Francisco, which allowed him eventually to receive his bachelor's degree and return to the halls of the university for a doctorate in jurisprudence and grammar.

There was no need for a royal pardon for Osuna. In the countries where Spanish is spoken, nothing ever happens to the bearers of great names, unless they entangle themselves with bearers of even greater names—and the poor slain soldiers were not that.

Neither the duke nor the poet was the sort to stay put: under the protection of the viceroy of Naples, they must have ranged farther. The allure of Rome at the turn of the seventeenth century was irresistible. No matter the day—October 4, 1599, included—anyone would have been better off in Rome than at a graduation ceremony.

First Set,
Third Game

When at last he could get up—his balls still throbbing like two melons with lungs—he walked over to the railing of the gallery and said in a faint voice to his second that he couldn't play like this: You have to do something. He rubbed his crotch gingerly. The duke, his eyes still brimming with tears of laughter, put a hand on his shoulder: You have to keep playing; Spain turns out nothing but soldiers and artists and you can't let anyone here know that you've never been to war. But it wasn't fair. You won the game, it was fair. So how am I supposed to move with a pair of octopuses for balls? Go and serve.

Holding the railing, he tried a few squats. Give me my sword, he said to the duke when, if not capable of playing, he at least felt capable of living. No, he's provoking you, the duke responded. Give it to me. I won't; it's Italian cunning, as if you don't know what they're like. I won't even unsheathe it; Spanish bluster.

The poet did one more squat, and when he rose, the duke was holding his sword belt over the railing. The moment the poet reached for his sword, Saint Matthew lunged for the artist's blade. The poet withdrew his hand and spat in disgust, stirring the spittle with the toe of his boot. He stared at the Italians as if they were creatures from another world, and then he returned to the line of service without giving them a second glance. All right then, said the duke, setting down the belt. With a half smile and a nod, the Lombard acknowledged that his opponent had recovered his dignity, and he moved to the rear of the court. The mathematician—who all this time had been counting the beams in the roof of the gallery—had fallen asleep. *Tenez!*

The first couple of points were played with force and fury (15–15). The artist was finally focused, and the poet had forgotten the encumbrance of his hangover and was intent solely on winning. The third point began with an extraordinarily vicious serve from the Spaniard, and the slice with which it was returned brought a moment of light to the court. Against the odds and perhaps the laws of gravity, the poet reached the ball as it bounced just inside the cord. His stroke was sound, but not forceful enough to win the point. He ran back, imagining that the artist would aim for the dedans; his guess was right. Then he covered the corners as if it were no work at all, his opponent peppering him with bullets, each harder, straighter, and deadlier than the last. At the end of the point the artist did something to the ball that killed it just as it cleared the cord. The linesmen exchanged glances: this might be a decent game after all. There was applause from Saint Matthew and the hangers-on, the two seconds, and the four or five people who had come to sit in the stands. *Quindici–trenta,* cried the mathematician; *primo vantaggio per il milanese.*

The poet noticed that the people still standing—maybe other

tennis players who would size one another up and take their measure against the poet's challenger when the professional gamblers began to arrive—were now finding seats in the gallery. The rapt interest with which the recent arrivals watched the movement of the ball gave him a tiny taste of glory, which, beleaguered as he was, he felt he definitely deserved.

It had been a difficult morning. He'd woken early with a parched throat and a headache hard and hot as a flatiron, and he hadn't been able to go back to sleep, confused, guilt-ridden, and mortified as he was.

What in Christ's name happened last night, he'd asked when the duke finally came down for breakfast at the Tavern of the Bear, where they were staying. The poet had been punishing himself for a while, sitting without a bite to eat on the plank floor of the courtyard, waiting for someone to come down and accompany him to Piazza Navona.

The duke's face was puffy and marked with pillow creases, but he was impeccably dressed in black: belt, cloak, and hat hung from his arm. Upon being asked what had happened, the grandee shrugged and called for a beer and some bread spread with lard. *Tiepida o calda*, asked the innkeeper's wife. Hot lard, warm beer—and put an egg in it. After his first swallow he opened his eyes a little more. His friend was still full of gloom. Nothing happened, he said, but we have to go and defend your honor, and mine too—the usual. The poet was conscious of his generosity in not even touching on the events of the night before. And Spain's, Duke, and Spain's. The other man smiled: Spain's indeed, when she's proved herself worthy. He finished the bread, gulped down the beer, and, rising, put on his gloves;

he fastened his sword belt around his waist and wrapped himself in his cloak. Let's go, he said, we can't be late.

Since it was nearly midday, the back gate to the courtyard was open and only the double doors separated them from the street. The duke put on his hat, opened one door, and looked to see who was passing before he set foot on the cobblestones—the hilt of his sword at hand, his fingers hovering nervously over it. He stepped out. Once on the pavement, he checked the street corners again and said: Clean and clear. But as he waited for the poet—who scarcely had the presence of mind to strap on his own belt—he kept his hand on his sword.

Tenez! Despite the complications of a serve set to rolling on the roof, the Lombard lifted the ball high enough to clear the cord, though with no sting. A survival stroke, one that left him off balance. The Spaniard hammered it back. Thirty–thirty. The next two points were long and exciting: many onlookers gathered. Deuce, cried the mathematician when they tied at forty.

A close, hard-fought game would be to the poet's advantage. To wear down the artist, he had to keep the score even. A tortuous and symmetrical match for an inclement day on which everything came in pairs. That morning the poet and the duke had walked to the piazza like Siamese-twin bailiffs. The two of them in cloaks and hats, shoulder to shoulder, right arms crossed over their chests. Spanish self-defense: fists visibly gripping hilts of swords. The people out to run a last errand before lunch had given them a wide berth. The inn wasn't far at all from the courts, and they made the walk without incident.

When the circus of Piazza Navona appeared before their nervous eyes, Saint Matthew and a few other louts were already in conversation by one of the L-shaped wooden galleries that bounded the courts the city had built so that the plebs could fortify their bodies and temper their souls—if they happened to have souls—by playing the fashionable game of the day. They moved toward the court, still on guard and with no sense at all of ridiculousness. Once arrived, they separated. The duke glanced at the Obelisk of Domitian, which in those days still functioned as a sundial. It's almost noon, he said.

The Italians, perfectly at ease, removed their hats when they saw them take their places in the gallery. Though the Spaniards were wearing swords—the pope had forbidden the citizens of Rome to bear arms—they were all cordial to one another, even warm, as strangers can be when they've spent a night drinking together. There were embraces, the duke's the most vigorous of all—the better to count daggers under capes.

The poet's opponent and his second appeared on the far side of the piazza a little later. The mathematician was dressed formally, like the poet and the duke, but in the blue robes and cap of a professor. He carried a leather case containing the implements of the duel. The artist, victim of a perhaps overly personal fashion sense, had on long, close-fitting black breeches of stiff, heavy cotton instead of hose. They fell to the heels of his boots. He was wearing a collarless shirt, also black, cinched by a leather vest of the same color. His cloak, cut in the Spanish style, was black and very worn. On his head was a narrow-brimmed hat, adorned with neither feather nor brooch. He carried a sword: his employment in the service of a bishop meant that this was permitted, even though he was a local.

For a moment it seemed as if the Spaniard would rally and

take the set. He went on the attack, covering the court like a man with a longer reach. When he didn't volley the return, he got to the ball after its bounce off the wall. The third time they came to a tie, the duke was happy to see that on the other side of the court a recent arrival had put his bet of four bits down on the service side. He noticed this when Matthew and his cronies, who until now had resisted the urge to bet, took up a collection of coins to put on the artist's side.

Custom dictated that the visitor choose a racket—one of two—and the ball with which they were to play—one of three—so the duke had been surprised that there was only one ball in the artist's kit. He took it. There was no substantial difference between the rackets, so he chose the one that seemed most used, thinking that it was probably the Lombard's favorite and that depriving him of it would put them ahead.

The contenders took off their cloaks and handed their swords over to their seconds. They would play in boots, since the pavement was uneven. When the duke took a coin out of his bag to toss for the serve, the artist shook his head and said in mangled but serviceable Spanish that he conceded to his guest. He spoke disdainfully—slouching and with his eyes on the gallery—but charmingly. When the shadow of the cross that topped the Obelisk of Domitian touched twelve noon on the cobblestones, the mathematician said solemnly and almost under his breath: *Partita*.

The Spaniard felt the leather of the ball between his left thumb and index and middle fingers. Once, twice, three times he bounced it on the pavement, spinning the racket in the grip of his right hand. He swallowed and rolled the ball again in the fingers of his left, looking at the ground, scraping the chalk line that marked the end of the court. With a shout of *Tenez!* he tossed the ball in the air and felt the catgut tighten as he lit into it with all his soul.

The artist had taken a magnificent stance, far back at an angle, his feet firm on the ground. He smashed the ball down just inside the cord. The Spaniard served again and lost the point again.

Cacce per il milanese, cried the professor. On to a fourth game, added the duke with some discouragement, but deep down he was excited, because the match was heating up and the spectators had begun to put money on the line. The poet watched the scramble to gather up coins. Maybe now you'll wager on me, he said to the duke.

Throat-slit

——— • ———

Rombaud's trial was so short that by the time the wretch understood what was going on, he had been sentenced. He had been seized for high treason at the very doors of the Salon Bleu and found himself unable to explain how he, a Frenchman and a Catholic, had offered his services as executioner to the heretic King Henry of England. In the death warrant, which was drawn up in haste and signed in a courtyard of the Louvre by Philippe de Chabot, it was written that the fencing and tennis master possessed the nobleman's right to have his throat slit without torture because the king had granted him privileges for life.

Lying on the ground, at the mercy of the soldier who was to perform the execution, the point of a sword pricking his neck, Rombaud wept. I understand, said Minister Chabot, that Anne Boleyn, a woman and a princess, didn't shed a single tear the day you dispatched her as she lay helpless; if you give me the fourth ball, he added, I'll let you go, and he motioned for the executioner to withdraw his sword.

The mercenary felt in his shirt and cloak and with shaking

hand extracted a lumpy ball, the most dubious of those made with the remnants of the queen's hair. Chabot put it in his pocket and said: Kill him.

The story must have traveled by word of mouth, since a bastardized version of it, based on elements of truth, lingered in the popular imagination. It's very likely that the episode, turned upside down like everything that crosses the Channel, lit the lamp of inspiration in William Shakespeare's head, since he chose to depict Henry V's unexpected claim to all the territory of France in a lovely scene that reproduces the handing over of the ill-fated Boleyn balls.

In the play's first act, King Henry receives a messenger from Louis of Valois, Dauphin of France, asking him to relinquish his claims to Normandy in exchange for the great treasure that he sends as a gift. The gift is a sealed barrel. The king asks the duke of Exeter to open it, and inside there are only tennis balls: a mockery of his political immaturity and lack of experience. Henry thinks it over and very coolly sends his thanks for the gift, saying: "When we have match'd our racquets to these balls, / We will, in France, by God's grace, play a set / Shall strike his father's crown into the hazard."

At the height of the Enlightenment, during an exchange of letters with Madame Geoffrin regarding the sale of his library to Catherine II of Russia, Denis Diderot describes how the preparations for his daughter's wedding have left him in a state of financial strangulation: "At first, my wife and I thought that the match would go some way toward easing the pressure of our creditors, and now we consider ourselves lucky if it doesn't kill us in the end. For me, Angelique's engagement has been the story of Rombaud's balls."

That very night, at the back door of his workshop, the craftsman who had made the Boleyn balls received a bundle of the mercenary's firebolt-chased chestnut hair.

The Ball on
the Right Is the
Holy Father

◆—•—◆

My balls are God and the King, and I play with them when I like. These words were part of Juana's only memory of her father. It was a flowery, tropical memory, necessarily remote: the old man had returned to Europe to petition for posts and concessions when she was five, and his lobbying was so long and fruitless that he died in Seville before he could return to what he thought of as his land. He thought this not because he had been born there, but because he was convinced that the whole place belonged to him.

Juana had reimagined the scene over and over again in her mind. The old man sitting on a stone bench in the infinite gardens of his palace—gardens that began in the valley of Cuernavaca and ended at some indeterminate point on the Isthmus of Tehuantepec. In her memory, her father's hair was already cropped and gray, but he still had the sinewy and arrogant spirit of those who've known power and have wielded it without qualms. He was a handsome and stubborn old man: eyebrows drawn together in an almost enlightened scowl of concentration, his beard a little dirty but tidy. He scratched his head as he listened to someone whom Juana could no longer bring into focus—his ragged nails burrowing in and out of the gray jungle of his sawed-off hair. He said to his aide: My balls are God and the King, and I play with them when I like. And he gave a tiny wave of his right hand, as if shooing away a fly. Then he turned to look at her where she must have been sitting, on another stone bench in the garden.

She remembered feeling something between adoration and fear at the seriousness of the forehead that had dictated countless death sentences with a movement of its eyebrows. The old man puffed out his cheeks, crossed his eyes. She laughed, maybe nervously. Then, with some effort, he got up and held out his hand to her. Let's go to the orchard, he said. Next, there was a long walk down a path into the world of fruit trees that her father had collected and that only the two of them knew by name, then the radiant moment when he lifted her up onto his shoulders and asked her to identify each in Nahuatl, in Spanish, in Chontal.

Many years later, when she was an adult, the duchess of Alcalá, and so far away from Cuernavaca that the memory seemed like someone else's, she asked her mother about the words she was sure she'd heard her father speak, whether they were really his or not. They had this conversation when she was pregnant with Catalina, her eldest daughter. The two women were sitting with their embroidery in the garden room of the villa of the Palacio de los Adelantados, their slaves and ladies in attendance, the orangish light from the north creeping in through the windows from which they'd had the latticework removed so that Seville would look a little like Cuernavaca.

The line about God and the King was indeed one of her husband's favorite sayings, the widow said, and he would utter it when one of his men or some priest dared to suggest that what he was doing might be improper for or unbecoming of a Christian. But the best part, her mother concluded, was the rest of it: The ball on the right is the Holy Father and the one on the left is the Holy Roman Emperor Charles V. Your father was an old bastard, she said in Nahuatl, to the delight of the ladies she had brought from Cuernavaca.

Juana didn't remember this extra bit that her mother recited with a laugh. The old woman thought for a moment and then said that Juana must have added "I play with them when I like," thinking that her father meant the balls for Basque pelota, which he played with other war veterans. And do you miss him, Juana asked, touching the belly in which Catalina was already splashing, the girl who in time would marry Pedro Téllez Girón, Duke of Osuna. Who? Father. He was old and rich by the time I had him, the poor thing; he imagined that he was a real nobleman and tried to behave like a gentleman. She laughed again, a bit hysterically, and said: He was a wolf in a fine cap. But did you like him? The widow opened her eyes wide and dropped her embroidery on her lap to underscore the drama of her words: Who wouldn't like him; he was Hernán Cortés, *se los xingó a todos*. Or, in Juana's polite translation for the benefit of the ladies and maids who didn't speak Mexican Spanish: He fucked everybody.

Game to
the Editor

◆—•—◆

From: Teresa Astrain <teresastrain@anagrama-ed.es>

June 12, 2013

To: Me

Subject: Second Pass

Álvaro, here are the files. One with corrections (just
a few) and a couple of queries. The other is a clean
version, for search purposes. For now it has the latest
title, handwritten. Too bad the subtitle is just one
syllable too long.

Now the ball is on your roof. Have at it.

Besos and onward,
Teresa

On 6/12/13 19:26, "Álvaro Enrigue" <aenrigue@gmail.com> wrote:

> Dear Teresa,
>
> Can I use this e-mail you just sent me in the new
> novel? As is. And tell me: Do you know where "the
> ball is on your roof" comes from? The novel—which
> you'll be seeing soon if Jorge decides he wants it—is
> all about balls and courts.
>
> Besos,
> Á.

On June 13, 2013 17:02, Teresa Astrain <teresastrain@
anagrama-ed.es> wrote:

> Somehow I knew that ball on your roof thing wasn't
> an actual expression. It means your turn.
>
> Please, please, please send the proofs back soon.
>
> Besos,
> Teresa

On 6/13/13 17:18, "Álvaro Enrigue" <aenrigue@gmail.com> wrote:

But you haven't answered my question, *cara* Teresa:
Do you know where it comes from?

The new subtitle should be "Dinero, letras y
cursilería." A little bit of tweaking and now it scans—
a perfect hendecasyllable.

Besos,
Á.

On June 13, 2013 17:23, Teresa Astrain <teresastrain@anagrama
-ed.es> wrote:

So we finally have a subtitle. I stayed late yesterday
playing with syllables, but I couldn't get it down to
eleven, not with all the accents in the right places.
You win. Now send the damned proofs.

Teresa

First Set,
Fourth Game

◆—•—◆

The Lombard was unstoppable at first, but then he got distracted. The score was love–30 when two women came by the court. They had just lunched and were dressed like what they were: whores. The Spaniard was so deep in the game that he didn't register their arrival. But his linesman sat lost in contemplation of them for a moment, because there was something familiar about these women and because they were truly fantastic pieces of tail. Despite the sporting rivalry between Italy and Spain on the tennis court, Osuna was sitting nearly shoulder to shoulder with the Lombard's linesman, so he could almost smell the women.

Without removing his gaze from their enticing skirts, the duke ran through the images he retained of the previous night. These two hadn't been at the brothel or the tavern. It took him a while to pinpoint where he'd seen them: in a painting that he'd had the leisure to examine as he and the poet waited endlessly for an audience with a banker. The whores appeared in it as models for Martha and her cousin Mary Magdalene.

The matter was resolved when he recognized a seductive flaw—a big mark like a continent on Martha's chin—which the painter had copied just as it was. They had even discussed it: Who would put a saint infected with some contagion in a painting? The poet had pointed out that Mary Magdalene, played by a strikingly lovely and spirited model, was holding the mirror of vanity in a hand with a crooked finger. The world turned upside down, he said.

Martha sat down next to Saint Matthew—an old cock among falcons—as if to calm the flurry that she and her friend had roused in the gallery. Meanwhile, Mary Magdalene, as defiant in the piazza as in her painted role of saint brought low by life, remained standing by the railing: her ass cocked, her cleavage a declaration of war. When she leaned forward, the duke noticed that the middle finger of her left hand was crooked. The artist who painted her hand hadn't twisted reality to suit the biblical tale, he had done the opposite: he had twisted the biblical tale by painting reality. The duke raised his eyes a little and fixed them on Mary Magdalene's breasts. He recognized them: they were, of course, the most defiant pair of tits in the history of art.

When the Spaniards had been received in the trophy hall of the banker's palace, they'd had a look at another eye-catching painting, in which the same woman—he hadn't realized it until just now, seeing her in person—appeared in a biblical scene, more jarring than the first, of a beheading in a bedchamber. The work was still propped on a chair: a place hadn't been found for it yet, lacking as it was in decorum.

It was an oil painting depicting the moment when Judith, having seduced the Assyrian general Holofernes, beheads him as he sleeps. The painting is bloody, but it also stirs up other things: in it, the model and courtesan looks more sensuous than vengeful as she slits the throat of the enemy of the people of Israel. She's seriously hot: her nipples are so hard that they show through her blouse, almost bursting out of it. The painting isn't a heroic portrayal of a Jewish nationalist committing the patriotic act of killing the oppressor of her people but the portrait of a killer who finds carnal pleasure in spilling the blood of the man whose semen still runs down the inside of her thighs. The odd look on her face isn't an expression of revulsion at the evil-doer overcome or disgust at having to behead him; it's an expression of pleasure: an orgasm.

Unlike the poet, who was still deep in the game, the artist let himself be distracted, and more: when the match permitted—and even when it didn't—he added his own shouts to the jests of the audience, making ridiculous flourishes to return the ball, blowing kisses to Mary Magdalene.

Cacce per lo spagnolo, cried the mathematician after the poet's last point, his fourth in a row since the arrival of the whores. The duke hurried onto the court to gather up his dividends from the line where the coins were stacked. It was a generous handful, the poet noted, because the professional gamblers were still mostly favoring the painter, even though the poet had a comfortable lead.

He didn't remark upon it to the duke, who put the coins in his pocket and then handed him a handkerchief to dry his sweat. He took his time fanning himself with the rag before beginning to wipe his torso. He even moved into the shadow of the gallery to put on the second shirt of the match, as gentlemen did. The Lombard was still wearing the same black shirt he'd had on since the night before, and very likely since the day he'd bought it. He was standing on the court, hands resting on the rail, just in front of Mary Magdalene, who was in the gallery; he had rested his head on her chest, as if accepting that his own body was defeating him.

Then, a long way off down the piazza, the duke's escort appeared. They approached the gallery with the clumsy, evasive humility of those who haven't been earning their pay. How goes it, one of them asked Osuna. We're winning; why don't you put a little money on our man, said the duke, because this is serious business. The men dug in their pockets without protest. The soldier of highest rank, Otero Barral by name, presented a pitiful fistful of coins. He was the smallest of the four, but possibly as a result, the scrappiest. Knobby and ruddy, he was the duke's favorite, because he could keep calm in any circumstance—the model of a certain type of Spaniard, specialized in persevering no matter what. Yesterday we spent like sultans, he whispered in excuse from behind his wolf-man beard. The duke shook his head, led him away from the court, and, when he was sure that no one could see them, gave him all the coins he had just won. He ordered him to hurry and put something on the line before the second set began. Otero looked at the money cradled in his hands and smacked his lips with undisguised greed. Put the thought from your mind, said his boss; we need the moral advantage. They returned to the gallery.

When he was back in his seat again, the duke noticed that the artist was watching Otero as he went to bet. He didn't remove his face entirely from Mary Magdalene's cleavage, but he was staring at the captain. He blew the hair out of his eyes, lowered his brows, sharpened one eye in a squint. It was a sticky look, which pierced Otero as he went about the insignificant business of bringing over the money, setting it on the line, returning to his seat. See how he watches Barral, the duke said to the poet; what can it mean—does he like his looks or does he want to start last night's brawl again? The poet shook his head. I don't think he even remembers what happened last night, he said.

Tennis, Art,
and Whoring

◆ • ◆

In the thirteenth-century work *The Book of Apollonius*, written in an early form of Castilian, the king of Tyre is blown off course by a storm and ends up in the city of Mytilene, where his daughter, Tarsiana, has been sold into slavery at a brothel and waits for someone to rescue her; like Scheherazade, she sings riddles that delay her surrender to the patrons.

When Apollonius and Tarsiana meet, they don't know that they're father and daughter, and she challenges him with riddles because he comes preceded by his reputation as a clever man, able to untangle any enigma. One of her rhymes, probably the oldest reference to tennis balls in Spanish, goes like this:

Hairy within and hairless without,
Tresses hidden deep in my breast;
I pass from hand to hand, always beaten about,
When the time comes to sup I sit bereft.

The tennis ball in *The Book of Apollonius* is described in a way reminiscent of the work that Tarsiana manages to stave off.

The ball is like a shaved woman—"hairless without"—that is hit—"always beaten about"—and that isn't invited to eat—"when the time comes to sup I sit bereft" because once it's been passed "from hand to hand" it's good for only one thing: to bounce around the piazza, making money for others.

Game to
the Author

—•—

On June 13, 2013 17:02, Teresa Astrain <teresastrain@
anagrama-ed.es> wrote:

Álvaro,

Please remember the book has to be ready before
summer vacation. Are you making any progress?

About the roof thing. What kind of question is that?
What kind of answer do you want? That it comes
from Latin? It must be based in real life: kids lose balls
all the time, balls end up on roofs, neighbors have to
throw them back. I don't know.

Return the proofs,
Teresa

On 6/13/13 17:19, "Álvaro Enrigue" <aenrigue@gmail.com> wrote:

No, Teresa: it comes from Renaissance tennis. The game was played on a court with a wooden-shingled roof over the spectators' seats. The serve had to hit it to be good.

Can I include our e-mails in the new novel if I send you the proofs by this weekend?

**On June 13, 2013 17:22, Teresa Astrain <teresastrain@anagrama
-ed.es> wrote:**

Great. I didn't know that. And I would prefer not to broadcast my ignorance, so please don't use my e-mails, and send the proofs by Friday regardless.

The Testament of
Hernán Cortés

—◆·◆—

The conquistador must have been a nice man, despite his unwieldy role as the protagonist in the greatest and most revolutionary epic of his century and possibly of all history. Something in his fate weighed heavily on him, bewildered him, set him apart from the world, and, possibly for that reason, he was very clear about everything else, to the last day of his life. Despite his bitterness, he was practically minded and funny. He hid his torments, which were many, behind clouded eyes that were not softened by old age.

He spent his final years far from the noble circles of Seville, where he would have been adored if only he had cared to behave a little and play along at court. But he was the kind of man who had seen so much that it would never have occurred to him not to scratch his ass if it itched.

He wasn't a hermit. At his house in Castilleja de la Cuesta he met regularly with the barber, the parish priest, the baker, the musician from the chapel, and a local poet—Lope Rodríguez— whose name has survived because he served as regular witness to the affairs of the conquistador. It was Rodríguez, it seems, who guided Cortés in the reading of classical epics, of which the conquistador was a fan so long as he didn't have to read them himself. He was probably already blind, but he was also a man who remained forever childish and somehow unformed. Like our children when they're little, he preferred to have someone read to him.

The conquistador was a one-horse man. When the horse upon which he entered Mexico City died at an advanced age in Seville, he buried it in his garden. From the day it could no longer bear him, he had refused any other mount. One gathers the beast was less a means of transport than the iron flail that increased a thousandfold the area of the Holy Roman Empire, but even so it's hard to imagine that when Cortés went to the city for provisions, he traveled in the priest's dusty cart or among the baker's baskets.

Lope Rodríguez, the bard, was with him on his last trip away from home, three months before death took him in his bed. We know the story because several letters survive, written from the poet to the widow left behind in Cuernavaca. Cortés went to see the Florentine banker Giacomo Botti so he could pawn the last batch of gems he had left in Spain, because he had no money to pay his doctor.

When he died, his belongings were auctioned off on the steps of the cathedral in Seville. The text of the "Tender of the Marqués del Valle," drawn up in September 1548 to certify the sale, included used clothing, a wool mattress, two stoves, two sheets, three bedcovers, a set of plates, a set of pitchers and copper pots, a chair, and two books. There isn't even a table or bed frame on the list: at the age of sixty-two he was still eating and sleeping like a soldier, though it's abundantly clear that he wasn't poor—his daughter Juana's dowry was more than enough to buy her the duke of Alcalá, who wasn't a bad catch for the child of an insubordinate.

The simplicity of Cortés's Seville possessions indicates something other than poverty: a spirit of retreat and a general disinterestedness; the fact that he was a man who no longer registered the material world, whether distanced by the memory of his momentary step into myth or by the resentment he felt for not having occupied a position of real bureaucratic power since Charles V—his left ball—made him a marquis and removed him from the captaincy of Mexico. It was only after he had been granted the title and returned to New Spain that he realized that this was a kick upstairs, that now he counted only as a millionaire.

Cortés's widow did play along at court when she eventually returned to Seville, but with an insulting lack of enthusiasm, and mostly to assure the future of her daughter Juana. There is nothing to suggest, however, that she was unhappy. When she left her palace of warmer days (and nights) in Cuernavaca and returned with Juana to Spain, she believed that she had done her duty to the world and she became a luxury object: a person who was invited places and kissed simply because she was someone the conquistador had fucked. She spoke in Bantu to her slaves, in Nahuatl to her attendants, and in Spanish to no one but her daughter—she merely smiled at everyone else, as if they were characters in a dream that had already gone on too long. She didn't fit into anyone's present because she was really an utter relic of the past: La Señora Cortés, Marquesa del Valle.

The sword, the lance, the helmet, and the arquebus that

would eventually hang on the wall of the garden room at the house of the duke of Alcalá had been kept by Lope Rodríguez after the conquistador's death, in the hope that Cortés's widow would send for him to bring them himself to the infinite palace of Cuernavaca.

Lope wrote a florid epistle, impenetrable and idiotic, to the marquesa del Valle, in which he suggested that she pay his way to New Spain so that once he had delivered the weapons he could give her a full account of her husband's pious last days. Along with the weapons, the bard had rescued the conquistador's scapular and the coat of arms that Charles V had granted Cortés, created according to a horrendous design that Don Hernán himself had proposed from Mexico.

"La Vermine
Hérétique"

——•——

Despite the enthusiasm with which King Francis received the Anne Boleyn balls, he never used them on court. He was a cultivated, sensitive man, given to secrecy, and though he made a show of satisfaction and mockery when they were presented to him, he never took them out of their box. It was natural in a man of his type, chilly and careful.

Francis I was not a creature of tennis courts and macho posturing. He had been a benefactor of poets and musicians, a patron of Leonardo; he collected books. When he was at last able to seize Milan from Charles V, he plundered all the classical art he could with rigorous benevolence and then lost the city again. His collections would be the foundation for what was later the Louvre—which he rebuilt—and the Bibliothèque Nationale. He financed the expedition of Giovanni da Verrazzano on which Virginia, Maryland, and New York were discovered, with no thought of expanding his realm.

It was in the city of New York that three of the balls made from the hair of the beheaded queen finally ended up. I saw them in the New York Public Library on Fifth Avenue at Forty-second Street, where they are kept in the archives of historic sporting equipment.

King Francis took the three balls to the Palace of Fontaine-bleau in 1536. There they remained, and never touched a tennis court, as the curator who is in charge of their care today explained to me. Most likely, he said with the air of someone who has spent much time thinking about something, they didn't spend long in the trophy hall before they were assigned a humbler and more honorable role as bookends. Were they removed even once from the box before they arrived in America? I ventured. Unlikely. Can I touch them? No. Why are they here? Andrew Carnegie bought them in a lot of French manuscripts and donated them to us; they arrived with the steel beams that hold up the ceilings of the library's underground stacks. I persisted: Is there any proof that they're the same balls from the box that Rombaud gave to Francis I? He pointed with his gloved index finger to an inscription on one of them in letters indecipherable to me: *"Avec cheveux de la vermine hérétique."* He translated for me, smugly: With hair from the heretic vermin.

Cortés's
Coat of Arms

———◆•◆———

Never has a man done for any faith what Hernán Cortés did for Renaissance Catholicism, and yet five centuries after the greatest religious feat of all time, the Vatican continues to look the other way whenever his name is invoked. What a provincial brute he must have been never to receive recognition for having set at the feet of the pope—his right ball—a world complete with all its animals, plants, temples, and little houses with hundreds of thousands of ladies and gentlemen inside, cavorting like rabbits, taking advantage of the fact that they could run around almost buck naked in the eternal good weather.

One has to see Cortés sweating in his armor, smoke-blackened and splattered by the blood of his enemies, imagine him blasting gods with his cannon. More than a soldier, statesman, or millionaire, the conquistador was the eye of a storm that hovered over the Atlantic for twenty-six years, its winds uprooting houses everywhere from the imperial Vienna of Charles V to the Canary Islands, from the Canary Islands to Tenochtitlan, from Tenochtitlan to Cuzco: one and a half million square miles full of people who sooner or later would become Christians because an uncredentialed man in his forties from the backwater of

Extremadura had broken the stewpot of the world without realizing what he was doing.

Each second, 4.787 people are born in Mexico, and 1.639 die, which means that the population increases by an average rate of 3.148 Mexicans per second. A nightmare. Today there are more than 117 million Mexicans, and an unspecified number followed by six zeros in the United States. A rough calculation suggests that between 1821, the year the country gained its independence, and the second decade of the twenty-first century, 180 million Mexicans, more or less, have been born. Out of all of them, only José Vasconcelos considered Cortés to be a hero. His unpopularity is nearly universal.

Take, for example, an inexplicable organization called the Mexican National Front, consisting of thirty-two skinheads. The thirty-two morons who belong to the Front are admirers of Hitler—and even they explain on their website that Cortés was a bastard. With the marquis del Valle we have a case of the most spectacularly bad image-management of all time. His last wish was for his body to be brought back to Mexico, where he wanted to be laid to rest. None of the 1.639 Mexicans dying at this instant visited his tomb; all would be opposed to a monument being raised to him, to his being memorialized on a plaque, to any object in the world reminding them of his existence. The 4.787 who've just been born will feel the same way. He did something very wrong, and he knew it: in his will he left alms for four thousand masses to be said for the salvation of his soul. If the masses, paid in advance, were said once a day in the parish church of Castilleja de la Cuesta, eleven years after his death his spirit was still being nervously commended each morning to the souls in purgatory.

All of this explains why no one in Mexico—or Spain either, I presume—has ever seen Cortés's coat of arms. It has four fields, the first of silver with the double-headed eagle of the Habsburgs representing the Holy Roman Empire, which the conquistador had expanded by dimensions too great to be calculated at the time. The second field is of sable, stamped with the three crowns of the Triple Alliance, which Cortés had overthrown when he subdued the Aztec empire on August 13, 1521, Saint Hippolytus's Day. A third is of gold with a lion celebrating Cortés's bravery, and a fourth of blue with a sketch of Mexico City atop the waters. Around the coat of arms is a kind of garland wreathing the four emblems, a chain from which hang the seven decapitated heads of the seven caciques of the towns of Lake Texcoco. Good taste was never Cortés's strong suit.

The coat of arms and the weapons never reached Mexico, because at the time of Cortés's death, the conquistador's daughter Juana was about to turn fourteen and her mother had already decided to return to Spain to find her a match in keeping with their infinite wealth—the worst possible scenario for poor Lope Rodríguez, who lost hope of any profit in the matter.

The Cortés ladies settled in Castilleja de la Cuesta and received the arms and the scapular in a solemn ceremony at which all the ragtag final companions of the conquistador were present, and which lasted about the time it takes to boil an egg. Then they focused their attention on making a marriage with the house of Alcalá, which didn't take much longer than the surrender of arms, because like all the nobles of Old Spain—as Juana Cortés dubbed the country that she was already beginning to find stifling—they were walled in by debt and clearly in decline.

Giant Heads

—◆—•—◆—

From the perspective of the Counter-Reformation Curia, preoccupied as it was with moral hygiene, Cardinal Francesco Maria del Monte had every imaginable fault. He was Venetian, he represented the sinister interests of the Medici and the French crown in the Vatican, and he was furnished with bottomless coffers that he basically used to corrupt everything—beginning with his own flesh. His list of friends included the major bankers of the city and a distinguished host of cardinals who could, if they chose, make life difficult for the pope. He was also proprietor of a noteworthy assortment of musicians, painters, poets, and castrati capable of circulating the most devastating gossip all over Rome. This confluence of power didn't make del Monte infallible—no one but the pope was infallible in those days of hard-line bishops and inquisitors with free rein—but he was tolerated to a nearly unique degree. His whims and pleasures far overstepped the incidentally rather foggy line of the acceptable, and even the legal.

Nevertheless, Cardinal del Monte died at a ripe old age, in possession of a moderate fortune—he lived well, but he wasn't a thief—and good humor. If he never became pope, it was only because the recently anointed Philip IV of Spain forced the vote from afar in the conclave of 1621 in order to close the gates of St. Peter's to the French crown. He lost the last Sistine round to Alessandro Ludovisi, who ruled as Gregory XV.

Despite all the power that del Monte accumulated, no visitor in the Rome of his day could say that he hadn't been received with courtesy and generosity at the Palazzo Madama, from which the cardinal manipulated Vatican politics with a silk-gloved hand for three decades; no one ever claimed that his operations—intrigue-filled and complex, given that he was the representative of the Medici grand duke of Tuscany in the city—had inflicted pain on a body or losses upon any coffers; and no one, absolutely no one, would have ventured to doubt his prodigious nose for objects of art that would increase exponentially in value.

If del Monte bought a work from a living painter and hung it in his celebrated music salon, the painter was assured inclusion on a short list of candidates for the decoration of an altar in the next chapel or a wall of the next cloister.

The art historian Helen Langdon has studied the collection of paintings amassed by Cardinal del Monte at the Palazzo Madama. The cardinal's Leonardos, Raphaels, and Michelangelos may have been copies, but he had five authentic Titians, a Giorgione, and several Licinios and Bassanos. And he was an enthusiastic collector of portraits, in imitation of the grand duke.

The inventory of his collections numbers more than 600 paintings—as well as ceramic pieces and sculptures—of which 277 were "unframed paintings measuring four palms each, of various popes, emperors, cardinals, dukes and other illustrious men and even some women." When he moved into the Palazzo Madama, del Monte contracted the services of the painter Antiveduto Grammatica—his real name—to supply him with copies of portraits. According to Giovanni Baglione in his *Vite de' pittori, scultori ed architetti moderni*, Antiveduto Grammatica was, in his day, "the great painter of heads."

It's likely that del Monte met Michelangelo Merisi da Caravaggio at Grammatica's workshop, where the artist labored during his years of poverty and obscurity, painting giant heads at piecework rates.

The majority of the portraits that adorned the walls of the Palazzo Madama are lost, and for good reason: they were junk, copies of copies made in the workshop of a talentless maestro whose name lives on only because it is associated with Caravaggio's youth. The few that it has been possible to identify show no sign of Merisi's master hand, whether because he didn't work on them—he wasn't Grammatica's only assistant—or because he turned them out mechanically, with no thought of proving anything to anyone. By then he was trying to make a place for himself as a painter with his own workshop, in the city that was the very navel of the art of his day, and he must have believed that investing effort in work that didn't even make him a good living was a waste of time.

What we are left with instead are several heads—not all of them gigantic—of Caravaggio himself. He appears in the grips of fever in *Sick Bacchus*, and stricken with anguish in the face of death in *The Martyrdom of Saint Matthew*. On May 29, 1606, he killed Ranuccio Tomassoni on a tennis court and was sentenced to death by beheading. Over the following years he painted his own severed head in two works: *David with the Head of Goliath*—which he sent to Scipione Borghese in return for pleading his cause before Pope Paul V—and *Salome with the Head of John the Baptist*—which he sent as a gift to the grand master of the Knights of Malta to request the protection of the order when the pope's executioners were closing in on him.

He had also painted himself as an adolescent in *The Musicians*, which he completed under the protection of Cardinal del Monte after he came to live on the lower floor—the servants' floor—of the Palazzo Madama in 1595. The lasciviousness of his half-open mouth, the succulence of his naked shoulders, the supplicatory look he gives the sole spectator of the painting—it was the first work that he painted for the cardinal's exclusive enjoyment—makes one imagine that he feels a gratitude that is at the very least voluptuous. In *The Musicians*, he portrays himself as a boy of fourteen or fifteen, though he was already a full-fledged and well-seasoned twenty-four when he painted it. This is unsettling, because during the talks of the conclave of 1621, the argument with which the representatives of Philip IV put an end to Cardinal del Monte's previously unstoppable campaign for the papal seat was that he ran a charitable mission recruiting boys of twelve or thirteen to be educated under his personal supervision in the palace. According to the cardinals' accusations, which are known because they were posted anonymously on the statue of Pasquino in Rome, del Monte recruited boys "not on the merits of their intelligence or neediness, but for their beauty."

There is a sixth head of Caravaggio, sketched ten or fifteen years after his death, in chalk on paper. It was done by Ottavio

Leoni, who knew him well. The brown of the eyes, the boldly drawn eyebrows that almost meet at the bridge of the nose, the untidiness of the rather thin beard, the unkempt and chaotic hair, the skin of the face shiny with grease, and the straight nose unblemished by age are the same as in his self-portraits, but in Leoni's drawing Caravaggio's expression isn't theatrical. He looks like what he probably was: difficult, peevish, ready for a fight. His right eyebrow, arched higher than the left, conveys irony and impatience, skepticism. The turned-down mouth signals that he was easily irritated; his slovenliness suggests that he was more arrogant than vain. Most of all, it is the saddest head ever drawn: that of someone already done for, caught in his own trap. The head of someone who no longer has a name of his own.

In March 1595, del Monte bought two paintings from the butcher and art dealer Constantino Spata, paintings by the young artist he had met in Antiveduto Grammatica's workshop of giant heads. It was so early in his career that they were still signed with the name of his Lombardy boyhood—M. Merixio—rather than the Romanized version of it, Michelangelo Merisi, which he adopted later, or Caravaggio—the town of his birth—with which he signed his works when he became famous.

The cardinal paid eight scudi for *The Cardsharps* and *The Fortune Teller*; four scudi each. In that same year of 1595, the artist Carracci sold his paintings for two hundred and fifty scudi apiece; del Monte's annual income—not the money he used for his political operations and the administration of the palace, but for his personal expenses—was one thousand scudi. It would have been enough to buy two hundred and fifty Caravaggios a year, twenty-one a month. In 1981, the Kimbell Art Museum in Fort Worth bought *The Cardsharps* for $15 million.

Despite his spectacular stinginess, Cardinal del Monte always knew exactly what he had bought. He unveiled the two paintings in the celebrated music salon of the Palazzo Madama, where they were so admired by his guests that he soon returned to Constantino Spata's butcher shop and bought *Sick Bacchus* and *Medusa*, which he sent as a gift to the grand duke. In the same fell swoop, carried away by enthusiasm, he bought Caravaggio too—fleshy shoulders, fresh mouth—and brought him to live among the servants of the palace so he could paint works on demand.

This was the turning point of Caravaggio's career, the moment when his life as an orphan adrift moved him onto the service side of the court.

Changeover

—◆—•—◆—

As it happened, the Lombard really didn't remember anything about the night before. Very likely he couldn't even remember each serve as he returned it, once the ball was in play. Maybe this was why he was enjoying himself so much during the break in a match where he had already lost the first set. The spectators had scattered about the gallery to stretch their legs, and some had gone to piss in the canal, so the painter, Mary Magdalene, and Matthew had a bit of welcome privacy.

Leaning on the gallery railing, he wasn't sure at all how he had come to be playing a Spaniard at tennis, nor why the Spaniard had an escort of soldiers, nor how he could possibly be losing when his opponent was a lame lordling with a face that drooped to the sides, like a pair of buttocks. Not that it mattered much: he was very happy breathing in the powerful scent of Mary Magdalene's tits as she asked him why the Spaniards could bear arms and his friends couldn't. They must be noblemen, said the Lombard, and he lowered his head, as if by sinking his nose into the whore's cleavage he could remove himself from a world that pressed on his temples and parched his throat. He inhaled. And those ugly soldiers, said the woman. The artist turned to look at them. He gave them a distant stare, his eyes nearly shut. They're green people, he said; except for their master, who's worse: pink as a pig. And he turned his attention back to her cleavage.

Matthew, who had been in a sulk for a while over the artist's disinclination to rapidly crush his opponent, noted that they were probably from the Naples regiment, but not soldiers. He added: They must be mercenaries, *capo mio*—as if he were morally superior somehow to a soldier, a mercenary, or anyone else. He was standing with his back to the court, next to his *capo*, who was now nuzzling Mary Magdalene's left clavicle.

If anyone associated with one of the families who ruled the city rabble had heard Saint Matthew refer to the tennis player as *capo*, he would have died laughing. The artist had the right to carry a sword because he was in service to a cardinal, which meant that he could make extra money by taking part in debt collection and street fights, but that was all. The flock of lowlifes who followed him everywhere wasn't a gang, though when bodies were needed they brought sticks and stones to the battle for control of a corner or a piazza. The *famiglia* that the artist belonged to took him seriously because of the lunatic ferocity with which he fought and because of his close ties to the cardinal, who protected him—he never had to spend more than a few hours in jail—but they didn't consider him trustworthy.

Saint Matthew scratched his ribs. Finally he said: Why don't we just give him a good beating? The artist sighed and sank his nose between Mary Magdalene's breasts again. They're Spaniards, she said; imagine the scandal. She said it in a dreamy way, her smile almost gentle, as if this imagined world weren't a feast of stabbings and throat-slittings, toward which it made no sense to hurl oneself. There would be war in the streets, she concluded, running her crooked finger across the artist's neck. If they're playing tennis with us they can't be very important, grunted the beggar. I tell you they're noblemen, it's risky enough to be playing tennis with them, Mary insisted. Win the match and put an end to it, *capo*, said Matthew. The artist shook himself a little, exhaled the rather stale air from his lungs into the tart's cleavage, and lifted his face. Shouting *Eccola!* as harshly as he might have called for a tavern to be opened at dawn, he went to get his racket and the ball he'd left lying on the pavement. Onlookers, gamblers, and friends found new seats in the gallery as the players changed sides.

Heavily and lazily, the Lombard went through the motions of crossing the court: dragging his feet, his eyes on the ground. Before he had settled himself on the defender's side, his second rose from his seat under the gallery roof, where everyone thought he had been sleeping, shook out his academic robes, and came to whisper something in his ear. The artist listened, his eyes cast down. For the first time that afternoon, his linesman appeared almost animated: he gestured as he talked. Finally, both of them kneeled on the ground and the mathematician drew lines, crossing some over others; he clapped once. The artist shrugged and the professor returned to his place in the stands to count beams.

The Lombard stopped behind the line, scraped the ground a little, and raised his face, in which a new demonic spirit shone. He half closed his eyes before crying *Eccola!* once again, this time from the depths where all the rage and violence of which he was capable was accumulated.

Admiralships and Captaincies

◆—●—◆

Neither the conquistador's widow nor his daughter Juana ever returned to Mexico, but they never developed much of an interest in the peninsular surroundings where they spent the rest of their lives either. Like all of Cortés's descendants, they found it inexplicable that infinite New Spain was dependent on this dim-witted country where men wore tights and screamed at each other even when they were in good humor. More languages were spoken in my father's garden than in all Old Spain, Juana would say by way of ungracious explanation of the little interest she took in Europe, where she had in fact been splendidly received. She didn't become a wallflower like her mother, who accepted every invitation and then was silent at the soirées, but nor was she notable for her devotion to the class to which she belonged by fortune and by marriage.

The decorous madness of the conquistador's widow made sense, in a way: she was already a grown woman when she left a kingdom of exceptional riches, where her orders were obeyed even before they occurred to her, but she had left it behind so that her daughter could be where one had to be if one was a woman. Her cool and at times even graceful distaste for her peninsular confinement was understandable.

Juana Cortés, on the other hand, lived in a fever of longing for America, because—having left Cuernavaca at fourteen—she never understood the body of war crimes that had made it possible for her to live her childhood like a native princess. The Andalusian orchards weren't bad, but one couldn't lose oneself in them, shed one's clothes deep in the wild, or play at spitting seeds and singing in Bantu with the slave daughters. The Guadalquivir wasn't the kind of river where heiresses to large fortunes swam stark naked after getting high on chocolate in the kitchen.

Once Juana Cortés had married the heir of the house of Alcalá, the conquistador's widow bequeathed his gloomy castle in Castilleja de la Cuesta to the religious order of the Descalzas and moved with her daughter to the duke's palace, which had an unbeatable name: Palacio de los Adelantados, or Palace of the Advance Men. The annual remittances that Martín Cortés was still sending her from New Spain were enough that she didn't have to worry about trifles like a private fortress on the outskirts of Seville.

In time, the Descalzas sold the conquistador's house to an Irish order of nuns, which still owns it and has seemingly incorporated into its cloistered existence the considerable penance of enduring the nightly siege of the four thousand lost souls vanquished by sword, lance, and arquebus that Don Hernán's dreams left plastered in the walls.

Juana Cortés was a Frida Kahlo *avant la lettre*: she wore

huipiles and multicolored skirts until the last day of her life, though she had left New Spain at fourteen and not a drop of Indian blood flowed in her veins. When she was required to attend functions of the Spanish nobility, she carried a coquettish little silver box of serrano peppers wrapped in a handkerchief, taking a bite of chili with each mouthful as if it were bread. She stressed the *s* sound of her *c*'s and *z*'s to signal her Atlantic origins. After all, she too was a product of the balls dubbed His Holiness and the King.

She clung to her father's weapons and coat of arms with the fierceness of a she-wolf, though the duke of Alcalá allowed her to hang them only in the garden room of the Palacio de los Adelantados, where the marks of Cortés's glory, won at the cost of hair and teeth, wouldn't overshadow the little prop weapons that encircled the Enríquez de Ribera coat of arms. She spent most of her life in that room, with her mother, both of them at work on their embroidery and striving to persuade the conquistador's granddaughters that their grandfather's virulent blood was the best part of them.

And it was easy for her to be arrogant: each time one of Juana's brothers—all of them named Martín Cortés, no matter what belly they came from—was hanged in New Spain for crimes of lèse-majesté, the chests of the house of Alcalá were filled to overflowing again.

Not infrequently, Juana lectured her daughters on her curious interpretation of their family names. According to her, the dukes of Alcalá were actually a clan of clerks. It was a bloodline that had maintained its ascendancy at court essentially by marrying off a daughter to a lord of Tarifa, with the subsequent acquisition of the admiralty of Castile. She arched her eyebrows as if to say that it was plainly a decorative title, considering the oceans—she pronounced it "oseanos"—of Castile. What was this compared with the territories that Cortés had won in a flurry of *xingadazos* for Charles V?

And frankly, for all of Cortés's many flaws, he is to this day the patron saint of malcontents, of grudge-bearers, of those who had everything and squandered it all. He is also the guardian angel of underachievers and late bloomers. He was no one until he was almost thirty-eight. At thirty-nine it occurred to him, from his perch on the Gulf coast of the Aztec empire in Villa Rica de la Vera Cruz, that his reconnaissance expedition should be a mission of conquest and settlement, and thus ruled by the king and the pope—his balls—and not by the idiot governor of Cuba, whose daughter incidentally was by then his first wife: he fathered a Martín Cortés on her too.

Three years after having defied the government of Cuba, he wasn't just Europe's greatest celebrity but the prince of all those who fuck things up without realizing it. He's the lord of the fight pickers, the litigious, those who can never acknowledge their own success; the captain of all those who win an impossible battle only to believe that it's the first of many and then sink in their own shit with sword raised. The conquistador wasn't the great man that the duchess sold to her daughters, but he was an inarguably more entertaining model than the landbound admirals on the other side of the family.

Juana Cortés's harangues always ended the same way: she pointed to her father's arms and said in Nahuatl: There is the sword that cut off the seven heads of the seven princes on the

Cortés coat of arms; let it never be forgotten, girls. Then she would return to her embroidery hoop, her thread, and her canvas, her mother seconding her with a series of rather alarming nods from her rocking chair.

This was more or less the atmosphere in which Catalina Enríquez de Ribera y Cortés, eldest daughter of Juana Cortés and the duke of Alcalá, and granddaughter of the conquistador, grew up. At sixteen she was married to Pedro Téllez Girón, Marquis of Peñafiel, future duke of Osuna, future defender of Ostend, future viceroy of Naples and the Two Sicilies, future pirate of the Adriatic, and future patron, comrade in revelry, and brothel mate of Francisco de Quevedo.

Paradise

—◆·◆—

Unlike the king and the rest of his court, Philippe de Chabot was a devotee not of art, culture, or tennis, but of the glory of France.

Ever since poor Rombaud had made an appearance in his rooms with a fourth ball made from the hair of the Boleyn woman, he had been thinking about the benefits that such an object might yield if placed in the right hands at the right time.

A ball made from the hair of the decapitated queen was the perfect gift for softening the already pliant Giovanni Angelo Medici, then governor of the Papal States, and a key piece in the negotiations with His Holiness regarding the urgency of forcing the succession of the marquisate of Fosdinovo in Lunigiana, where one Pietro Torrigiani Malaspina, patron of mediocre artists and magnificent thugs, was blocking the loading of marble onto French ships in the port of Carrara.

The ball couldn't be sent to Rome as it was, so he had a little chest made from sheets of mother-of-pearl riveted with gold, which in addition to matching the regal sumptuousness of its contents had the advantage of being a lengthy job for the goldsmith. This allowed the minister—who was a devotee of the glory of France but also (though always secondarily) of the delectable sexual practices of low-ranking and high-breasted courtesans—to embark on a bedroom game or two with the ball, beneath whose leather stays beat Anne Boleyn's incendiary braids.

Flight to Flanders

◆—•—◆

Catalina Enríquez de Ribera y Cortés and Pedro Téllez Girón had not just a marriage but a powerful business partnership in which each provided the other with what was needed to act on a grudge. He brought new visibility to the gray house of Alcalá with his political savvy and his proximity to the king; she contributed money and the memory of the wiles of her grandfather, who had gone away and won what he believed he deserved.

When Osuna learned that a detail of bailiffs was being sent from Madrid to arrest him for abusing the generosity of the king with his trip to Italy, he set off for Ostend. He left for Flanders by night, accompanied by a single servant. There he joined the royal regiments like any other soldier until he was distinguished by his valor in combat.

The house of Osuna had no precedent for this: fleeing the king by taking up arms to defend the king; fighting bitterly to reclaim a territory in order to win a royal pardon; forcing the monarch and all his judges and bailiffs to pay obeisance. The only thing he carried with him on the jaunt was Cortés's sword, which Catalina took down from the wall of the garden room and gave to him before he set off on the road like a bandit.

There were likely few husbands in Spain at the end of the sixteenth century who were as unfaithful as Osuna, and it's interesting to note that each time the young duke was put under house arrest for reasons to do with his capacity for drink and the ubiquity of his member, Catalina had to embrace the sentence and serve it with him.

Many years later, at the fateful hour of the final and most serious of the duke's confinements—the one that spelled his end because this time he was accused of lèse-majesté and his enemies at court were infinite—Catalina Enríquez de Ribera y Cortés didn't hesitate to write a spectacular letter to Philip IV in defense of her husband. Addressing the king with the familiar *tú*, the duchess reminded him that his Holy Roman Emperor great-grandfather, Charles V, had treated her grandfather Hernán Cortés as wretchedly as he was now treating Osuna. She reminded him that Ostend would have fallen and Spain given way to the Low Countries entirely had it not been for her husband's defense of the city—which was true, to a certain extent. She pointed out that because her man had fought in the mud to defend the king, Spain had been able to sign a treaty rather than concede defeat.

The letter didn't sway Philip: the duke died under strict house arrest on September 20, 1624.

The night of November 26, 1599, when Osuna had fled to Flanders, his wife had accompanied him to the door of the Palacio de los Adelantados—where both had hid while the king's bailiffs called for him at his own palaces. Stay alive, she said before giving him a kiss. She touched his chest. Are you wearing the scapular? He felt it under his shirt. Don't take it off.

The Banker and
the Cardinal

—◆•◆—

Though Cardinal del Monte was Caravaggio's official patron in the years when he burst onto the scene of Mannerist painting in order to annihilate it, del Monte wasn't the primary collector of his paintings. He had the discernment to discover him, but not to understand what he would be capable of once he set about painting with absolute freedom and support, as he did once he had a studio at the Palazzo Madama and enough commissions to unleash his visual experiments. Back then, his brilliantly colored paintings must have looked very strange, with characters from sacred history portrayed as the lowly beings who crowded Rome at the end of the sixteenth century.

The banker Vincenzo Giustiniani, head of the Repostaria Romana and principal financier of the French crown, must have seen Caravaggio's paintings in the Palazzo Madama's music salon—he was a neighbor and good friend of Cardinal del Monte—and without ever encroaching on the cardinal's patronage, he bought up all the works by the artist that were perhaps too scandalous to hang in the house of a prelate. These works—possibly too extreme for del Monte not only to display but even to understand—turned out to be plentiful. At the end of Merisi's life, the cardinal had eight of his paintings and the banker fifteen.

Caravaggio's work was just one of the realms in which del Monte and Giustiniani competed for objects that skirted the acceptable in Counter-Reformation Rome. If del Monte bought the second telescope produced for commercial purposes by his protégé Galileo Galilei, it was because Giustiniani had bought the first. At the cardinal's grand parties, just as at the banker's more spartan gatherings, the high point was always the moment when someone opened the door to the terrace and invited the guests to see the moon from as close up as the Selenites must have seen it.

Del Monte and Giustiniani couldn't have been more different. The banker was a married man, terribly bored by the worldly obligations of his work as financier to the pope. When he could, he escaped to the scrubland of Liguria to hunt deer and wild boar. He was long and gaunt, with the kind of sharp face that betrays the true predator. He spoke little and read a great deal. Nothing could have been more unlike the cardinal's gelatinous exuberance. The two men's friendship—in addition to being genuine—was a fire-tested bond that made it possible for them to operate comfortably, though because of their French connection they were always in the minority at the Vatican.

Both were lovers of mathematics and sponsors of treatises on the mechanical sciences. Both invested time and money in a novel form of alchemy that didn't seek the transmutation of metals or the elixir of youth but rather a knowledge of the essential elements of the earth—what we now call inorganic chemistry.

Anyone who believes that earthly objects are all composed of the same group of substances, and that transformations are accomplished only by mechanical means, will naturally perceive the voice of God in the filthy fingernails—nails that are of this world, a part of history—of Caravaggio's saints and virgins. The voice of a god more brilliant than capricious; a god unlike God, remote and uninterested in revealing himself in miracles beyond combustion or the balance of forces; a true god for everyone: the poor, the wicked, the politicians, the rent boys, and the millionaires.

Caravaggio was to painting what Galilei was to physics: someone who took a second look and said what he was seeing; someone who discovered that forms in space aren't allegories of anything but themselves, and that's enough; someone who understood that the true mystery of the forces that control how we inhabit the earth is not how lofty they are, but how elemental. Del Monte and Giustiniani surrendered to Caravaggio. For the banker, it was the paintings; for the cardinal, the man. The two of them lived in palaces that faced each other across the piazza, at the end of which was the church of San Luigi dei Francesi, where Merisi's first public works of art hang.

At the time of his leap to fame, the artist never had to walk more than three hundred yards to deliver the painting he had just finished.

Second Set,
First Game

◆—•—◆

The serve fell within easy reach of the Spaniard, who risked aiming straight for the dedans even though the Lombard was planted right in the middle of the court. The artist's backhand return was flat-out impossible not only to stop but even to see. The ball struck in the corner, inside. *Quindici–amore*, said the mathematician, but it sounded like a titter. Easy, that's not the way, shouted the duke. The poet understood that when he was on the receiving side it was impossible to surprise his opponent—that he needed to wait him out.

He took the artist's second serve off the roof, and quickly moved up to the center of the court. Here he was able to contain a drive from the left, but the next shot blazed from the right. Impossible to reach. The duke, whose eyes had been popping out of his head ever since he saw the buffeting the poet took on the last point, didn't even bother to try to call out the score. *Trenta–amore*, the professor almost whispered.

The Lombard had woken in a splendid mood that morning, even though his first glimpse of dawn came when his second dragged him off his cot by his foot. He had fallen flat on his ass on the clay floor, its cool contact with his buttocks faintly pleasurable. Then he scratched his head with both hands. All right, he said, still a little drunk, and he rubbed his belly with his right hand and worked his still-swollen face with his left. Then he scratched his pubic hair, massaged his temples, and only then opened his right eye a crack—the left was sticky with sleep.

The professor, already dressed and washed, had glanced rather greedily at the artist's rock-hard erection, the result of his spell lazing in bed. He sat down next to him. We're late, he said, brushing bits of mattress straw from the painter. Rouse yourself; last night we agreed to a duel. A duel? The painter's mouth was pasty, with an acrid taste of grease from the fried tripe he'd eaten before turning his attention to the barrel of grappa the night before. The mathematician stroked his abdomen, still ridged as a grill, traced the trail of hair that began at his navel, then removed his hand. The artist wiped the sleep from his left eye with a finger. Don't you remember? No, but if I kill anyone just now my head will roll. It's a game of tennis, the professor explained; against a Spaniard. The artist closed his eyes and raised his eyebrows, worries gone. He rested his head on the bed, rocking it back and forth. He scratched his neck. Did we fuck last night, he asked the professor. You drank so much you'd never have got it up. But did you? Yes. Well, then, you owe me. He stretched his legs. The professor understood what this meant and obeyed the demands of the painter's member, stroking it slowly. So did I enjoy it, asked the artist, still with a half smile. Instead of laughing, the mathematician snorted, and the artist stretched his arms along the edge of the mattress, parting his legs a little and closing his eyes. He rubbed his buttocks on the cold floor so that the pleasure spread to his spine. The professor put the point of his nose in his ear; when he felt the base of the artist's member swell he squeezed his testicles gently. The artist came, more tenderly than forcefully. As he did so, he clung to the professor's neck. Hold me. We have to go. A moment, no more.

The professor let his cock sleep in his hands, then he got up. Only then did the artist open his eyes and look at him. The mathematician felt that he was taking the measure of his skull. He ran his hands through the artist's hair to wipe the pollution from between his fingers. Are you going to let me paint you? Now the Lombard was stroking the professor's slack sex with the tip of his nose and his chin. The mathematician was in his formal robes, so it was more a gesture of gratitude than an invitation to keep playing. I'm not your whore. He let him go on a little longer and then said: I'll wait for you outside; we swore very solemnly last night that we would be there. The artist slapped his thigh as if to say that now he was really getting up.

For breakfast he had half a bottle of wine that he found at the foot of his cot—he imagined the mathematician must have left it there when he went off the night before to the sumptuous palace guest rooms, where he slept when he was visiting Rome.

Two more slams and the game was the artist's in a shutout. The Spaniard never found a spot where he could block the shots of such a versatile foe. The Lombard had risen like a hawk over the match, exercising graceful but firm control of the henhouse in which everyone else around the court flapped. He was playing so well that he didn't seem to even be trying, or particularly possessed by the spirit of victory, let alone hungover, sleep-deprived, and raped by a mathematician. He was unimpeachable, nearly perfect. He's playing like a saint, the Spaniard said to his second at the break. Before he returned to the court, the duke said: Wait, and from around his neck and under his shirt he drew a scapular. He hung it around his companion's neck. It's very good luck, he said. What is it, asked the poet, eyeing the faded image. A Mexican virgin, I believe; incredibly good luck.

The escorts lost the coins they had bet. Their master gave them more, eyes on the player done in by the sun and the shock, his shoulders down around his hips in pure defeat. Bet on points, not games, the duke said to Otero; maybe then it'll be less of a bloodbath. With all due respect, the mercenary replied, I don't think how we bet will make any difference.

Middle Class

◆—•—◆

POSTS OF PEDRO GÓMEZ, QUEVEDO'S FATHER
Scribe to Maria of Austria, Holy Roman Empress
Chamber Scribe to Anne of Austria
Chamber Scribe to His Serene Highness
   Prince Charles
Chamber Scribe to His Highness

**POSTS OF JUAN GÓMEZ DE SANTIBÁÑEZ,
QUEVEDO'S PATERNAL GRANDFATHER**
Chamber Scribe to Their Highnesses
Gentleman-in-Waiting to Anne of Austria
Gentleman of the Bedchamber to Our Lady Queen

**POSTS OF FELIPA DE ESPINOZA, QUEVEDO'S
MATERNAL GRANDMOTHER**
Lady of the Queen's Wardrobe to Her Majesty
Lady of the Queen's Toilet to the Infanta Isabel

Weddings

—◆•◆—

Juana Cortés didn't attend her daughter Catalina's wedding to the duke of Osuna: she found it irritating that the king was among the guests. Her gift to her daughter was a jade necklace inscribed in Latin that had been the conquistador's wedding present to Catalina's grandmother. The necklace is lost, like most Cortesiana.

She summoned the duke the day before the start of the festivities. She told him that when she died, the conquistador's arms would go to him because none of the Martín Cortéses were foolish enough to return to Spain. Then she reached out her madwoman's hand, for a moment the nest of all past and future misfortunes of the vast Americas, and in her palm was a little matte-black sparrow, framing an image so worn it was unrecognizable. It's Cortés's scapular, she said; my gift to you. The duke opened his palms to receive it like the Communion host. It wasn't as if he believed the tales about his betrothed's infinite grandfather, but he understood that the woman was bequeathing him a soul. The scapular was made with hair cut from the head of the emperor Cuauhtémoc after Cortés had him killed, she said; may it protect you—my father never took it off, and he died of old age with more lives on his hands than anyone before him. Osuna looked at it, feeling something between fear and disgust. Put it on, said the old woman.

The duke never said much about the afternoon he spent with Juana Cortés on the eve of his wedding, but he came out of the garden room in a different frame of mind: more serious, and somehow liberated. He had learned that there's no point worrying about one's fate, because all paths lead to defeat: nothing is ever enough for anyone.

That night he took the scapular out from his shirt to show Catalina. They were bidding each other farewell after dining with the family members who had arrived at the Palacio de los Adelantados to attend the festivities. She looked at it with surprise. Odd that she gave it to you, she said. The duke shrugged his shoulders. It's a horrible thing, really, he replied. It was a rectangle woven of very fine, strong black thread. Worked into it was a figure that could no longer be identified. What is it, he asked his betrothed. A virgin of Extremadura, the Virgin of Guadalupe; the Indians made it for him; if you put it up to a candle it shines with a light of its own. Osuna approached a candelabra and couldn't see anything. He tilted the scapular until the slant of the light made it glow: immediately he recognized the figure of a virgin in a blue robe, surrounded by stars. So brilliantly iridescent was the thing that the image seemed to move. He let it fall, frightened. Will it burn me? Don't be an idiot, his future wife said. She took it and made it shine again. It looks like this because it's made of feathers, she explained. Feathers? Bird feathers; that was how they made the images, so they would shine.

He tucked the scapular back into his shirt. He had to go and rest before the banquets began. He bowed. Before he could retire, Catalina asked again what he had spent so long talking to her mother about that afternoon. Your grandfather, a huge garden, Cuernalavaca. The future duchess corrected him: Cuernavaca. I'll walk with you to the hall, she added. They went down the stairs arm in arm. As they were approaching the door where they would part for the last time before they were married, Osuna asked with sincere and perhaps slightly alarmed curiosity: So what does it mean to *xingar*, would you say?

A Council Is
Wagered and Won

———◆•◆———

G iovanni Angelo Medici was a practical man. The son of a
notary from the north of the Italian peninsula with no ties
whatsoever to the family of the grand duchy of Florence, he
governed the Papal States with diplomacy, restraint, and a low
profile: qualities valued in the Renaissance era, which it was his
lot to bring to a close. He greatly appreciated the gift that he
was sent by his friend and counterpart, Philippe de Chabot,
minister plenipotentiary for Francis I of France. He kept the
fourth Boleyn ball in his desk, tossing it from hand to hand
when he received someone with whom he had complicated business, as if to suggest that they should wrap things up quickly.

Just a few years after Giovanni Angelo Medici received the
ball, his elder sister married a brother of Pope Paul III, and now
nothing could slow his rise up the ecclesiastical ladder: he was
the only member of the Curia who maintained equally smooth
relations with the king of France and the Holy Roman Emperor
Charles V of Spain.

In 1545 he was named archbishop of Ragusa and in 1549 he
became a cardinal. All this despite the three conspicuous illegit-
imate sons who accompanied him everywhere. Ten years later,

he was elected Pope Pius IV. He was appointed as a compromise, certain to last only a short time in the Vatican seat—here, too, he failed to heed expectations.

In addition to being a great manager, a politician untouched by defeat, and a bulldog for the election of his allies, Giovanni Angelo Medici was a lover of tennis. Even when he was pope he played senile doubles matches with his sons, and before that, when he was head of the Papal States and bishop of Ragusa, he was often seen at street games of *pallacorda*, red with enthusiasm and betting heavily on his three young bucks.

Relaxed to the point of corruption with his friends, implacable in the pursuit of his enemies, charming even when issuing death sentences, Giovanni Angelo Medici was the key figure in the transition to the Counter-Reformation and its splendid Baroque art.

In 1560 he named Carlo Borromeo bishop of Milan, making him the new model for the high clergy: he was curt and lean like a Franciscan but possessed a sophisticated education and was capable of navigating the turbulent waters of court receptions unscathed. Borromeo was an insufferable fanatic, but he was also very charismatic and never demanded anything of anyone that he wouldn't do himself, which meant that he was the most persuasive of the agents of the new morality and the new aesthetic, dripping with the asceticism and glassy-eyed stare demanded by an age of great ecclesiastical revolution.

Pius IV named Carlo Borromeo bishop of Milan because of the great shrewdness he had shown in his first assignment as papal secretary. It was an undertaking that until his appearance was deemed hopeless: restarting talks at the Council of Trent.

In the ten years during which Trent was on hold, the disagreements between the Spanish and French cardinals had become so extreme that the only way of bringing them back together was to promise that the Council would begin again from zero. It was no wonder: this was the decade when Charles V quit his position as the most powerful monarch of all time, leaving the Holy Roman Empire split in two and the throne of Spain under the buttocks of his son Philip II, who never understood that the whole business of the defense of Catholicism was a charade. The king of France was a Protestant boy who had converted to Catholicism solely for political reasons. England and the northern principalities of Germany, whose cardinals had attended the first session of the Council even though they had already broken with Rome, had simply lost interest; they were perfectly happy being simply Christians, and even turning a profit from it. There were no cardinals who could mediate between the envoys of the new kings of Spain and France.

Carlo Borromeo convinced both parties that Pius IV would wipe the slate clean once they sat down around the table at Trent. At the first session His Holiness began, "As we were saying yesterday . . . ," and the discussion grew so heated so quickly that on the second day, when the pope insisted that they start from scratch, the cardinals rebelled and demanded that they follow the order of the day as they had left it the previous afternoon.

The council's final act was no less politically deft. When Borromeo and Pope Pius judged that the cardinals were simply going around in circles, the office of His Holiness—without informing anyone beforehand—released a bull, *Benedictus Deus,* which listed the council's conclusions and urged bishops everywhere to submit to its dictates.

There were, of course, mutinous cardinals who wanted to go on with the talks. There were even some who refused to accept that sensitive questions should remain open, to be codified later in a new catechism. Pius wore them down with pastries, wine, meaningful smiles, and, to be frank, barely veiled threats: never since the Rome of the Caesars had so many ditherers been executed. I believe, said Pius IV to those who refused to sign his acts—this after feting them marvelously—that you should speak to our dear friend Cardinal Montalto.

Montalto was the most bloody-minded of his inquisitors, the most bitter opponent of seeking everyone's agreement—Utter hogwash! Is there not a captain aboard the ship?—and the most fervent defender of the idea of finally writing a catechism that would allow him to burn all Europe at the stake.

Borromeo wouldn't have been opposed to the idea. Pope Pius IV couldn't have cared less, so long as he could watch the conflagration from the comfortable vantage point he enjoyed as last pope of the Renaissance: listening to music, eating well, enjoying the company of friends.

Ball Games and
the Ancients

———•———

The Romans played four kinds of ball games: *follis*, *trigo-nalis*, *paganica*, and *harpastum*. *Follis* was the game of large and small balls inflated with air; the large ball was hurled by naked players, their fists clad in metal up to the elbow, the whole body smeared with clay and oil—an unguent they called *ceroma*. Another was called *trigonalis*, whether because the room in the baths where it was played was triangular, or because the players were three. The third was called *paganica*, because it was played by the villagers, who in Latin were called *pagani*: now the ball was of cloth or leather, rather loosely filled with wool, feathers, or hair. The fourth and last game, *harpastum*, was played with a very small ball on a dusty floor. None of these ball games exist any longer. Instead, leather balls tightly packed with hair are played with sticks. There is a ball inflated with air that is used in Flanders and Florence and it is called *va-lone*, and there is the racket, very much employed in Rome.

Letter from LICENCIADO FRANCISCO CASCALES *to* FATHER
M. FR. FRANCISCO INFANTE *of the Carmelite Order,* 1634

Giustiniani's
Studiolo

◆—•—◆

The vagaries of sixteenth-century Mediterranean politics made Vincenzo Giustiniani, heir to the all-powerful banking house of San Giorgio in Genoa, a poor boy. The Turks had invaded the island of Chios, property of his father and seat of the Giustinianis' financial empire, and, along with the land, his family had lost absolutely everything. Shattered and destitute, they had gone to Rome when the future banker was two years old.

The Giustinianis of Genoa had been the main financiers of the Spanish empire and had swung bloodily and without warning from extreme opulence to utter helplessness, the common state of immigrants in Rome. To make matters worse, they arrived stigmatized as *conversos* because working in finance was so reviled at the time. In the portrait that Nicolas Régnier painted of Vincenzo Giustiniani in the 1630s, a trace remains of that stigma: his face is endowed with a nose so extreme that it nearly covers his mouth.

In time, Vincenzo's father recovered his fortune and perhaps even increased it—his new clients, who were the Crown of France and the Vatican, were more reliable payers than the

Philips of Spain. But to do so he had to embark on a regimen of work and savings that shaped his sons' sense of professional discipline—Vincenzo's brother, a priest, was the pope's accountant—as well as political affiliation: they never forgave Philip II for failing to offer them asylum in their hour of need for fear of being called a *converso*phile.

This is why it's so disconcerting for historians that Pedro Téllez Girón, Duke of Osuna, paid Vincenzo Giustiniani an unexpected visit at the end of September 1599. Likely Girón, weary of being hounded by King Philip, believed that he could spark some kind of alliance that would restore luster to his house—a luster long lost, to be frank, and for which the fortune that had come to him by marriage was a respite but not a safe haven. Maybe he had already decided by then that when he was back from Rome he would go to Flanders to fight, and he dreamed of mustering an army with a capital greater than Catalina's. Or maybe he was simply seized by nostalgia for the years when his father had visited Chios to negotiate the loans that allowed Philip II to build mines in New Spain and Peru.

It was at the Palazzo Giustiniani that Pedro Téllez Girón learned that the dazzling painting of the calling of Saint Matthew that he'd seen at the church of San Luigi dei Francesi had been done by an artist without a proper name, who was known as Caravaggio.

Osuna hadn't the slightest intellectual tendencies. His loyalty to Francisco de Quevedo is a mystery that can be explained only by the fact that the poet, so cerebral and unyielding, also had—when he wasn't translating Latin verse or writing treatises—a rakish and swaggering side as powerful as his monster brain.

With the years and the investment in bribes made with his wife's money, Pedro Téllez Girón became a politician graced with pen-pushers and pettifoggers who wrote his letters for him, but in the autumn of 1599, when he was received at the Roman offices of the bank of San Giorgio, he wasn't in correspondence with anyone, nor did he keep written records of anything. It's likely he was a functional illiterate and this was precisely why he dragged his personal poet along everywhere—though Quevedo didn't take notes either. There is no record of the meeting between Osuna and Giustiniani other than a note by an anonymous secretary, who on September 28 of that year wrote in the guest book of the palace on Piazza di San Luigi: *"Visita di P. Girone, nobile e fuggitivo spagnuolo."* And then it is recorded that he was received in the trophy hall, which suggests that the banker had no intention of doing business with him.

The Palazzo Giustiniani was as sober as its owner. In any other residence of this type there might be tapestries and taffetas, but here there were only bookcases; where there might have been long rugs and cushioned chairs, the banker had terra-cotta and tile floors and uncomfortable Savonarola chairs. If at palaces like Cardinal del Monte's there were endless galleries hung with paintings from floor to ceiling, in Giustiniani's house the paintings were separated by blank stretches of whitewashed wall that must have given his visitors agoraphobia.

Of all the works that made up his legendary collection of art, the only one allotted its own room—the *studiolo*, separate from the bank's office—was Caravaggio's *Judith Beheading Holofernes*. He had it behind a curtain, which he opened before sitting down to eat or work and closed when he left, as if the gaze of the servants who cleared the plates or swept the floor might wear it out. If Osuna and his poet were very lucky, they might have seen it, since before it came to rest on the secular altar where he hid it away, Giustiniani kept it in the trophy hall, another space off-limits to the women and children of the household.

Second Set,
Second Game

—◆•◆—

To say that in the second game the artist crushed the Spaniard is an understatement. The poet could hardly carve out a point despite the superhuman effort with which he chased the ball, trying desperately to take the sizzle off his opponent. The Lombard floated on the service side with the implacable grace of a clock made of flesh. During the changeover an aura of precision and strength had settled about the painter, leaving the poet certain of being a simpleton, a laggard, a newcomer to every fight. He felt dull, aged, unctuous, more Spanish than ever, and so conscious of his lameness that it seemed the whole universe: his right leg was short a third of a span and that third was where the painter was putting the ball over and over again. It wasn't that he was doing anything wrong: the artist had simply been seized by one of his spells of perfection. *Quaranta–quindici*, the mathematician cried again. The duke had forgotten by now that he too had the right to call points and even dispute them: his mouth was good for nothing but swallowing saliva.

The mathematician wasn't a creature of tennis courts or street fights. Nor was he in the habit of sleeping with men. At the palace of the sodomite cardinal in whose rooms he stayed when his work brought him to the papal city, he scratched an itch. That was all. That and the fact that the artist who lived and worked in the depths of the palace had shifted something in his center of gravity ever since he was introduced to him as the cardinal's most recent acquisition. He found him at once brutal and vulnerable, fragile behind his armor of grease, grappa, and cussedness. He loved that the artist was an unfinished man; a contradictory creature who might just as easily call for another drink after exchanging blows with a stranger in a brothel as—when they returned to the palace late at night—prostrate himself on the floor to remove the mathematician's boots and run his tongue devotedly along the curve of his foot. He had never met nor would he ever meet anyone so extreme, even though in the difficult years when he was persecuted by the Inquisition he would be questioned a thousand times by the world's most perverted priests. Nor was the professor especially particular in the exercise of his sexuality: he believed that in terms of texture and pressure there was little difference between the cunt of a sheep and the ass of the greatest artist of all time, so he might as well fuck him in the name of scientific experimentation.

And there were the paintings. He had never seen anything like those paintings, whether in Pisa, where he was born, or in Florence, where he completed his studies, or in Padua, where he taught and kept a wife who differed little from a sheep or a great artist except that she gave him children.

It was as if the full spirit of the age had its home in the artist's fist: the darkness, the aridity, the bleak dignity of empty spaces. When he had come to Rome the year before to sit an examination for La Sapienza, the mathematician had confessed to the cardinal that he would rather stay at the University of Padua: Rome is a gap-toothed city, he said; full of vacant plots, half empty like the canvases of your painter.

The professor came from a family of the Tuscan petty nobility. His father was a mathematician, too, but refined by the abstractions of music rather than the coarseness of materials and their movements: he was a lutenist. He and del Monte had become friends at seminary, where both of them played in a papal orchestra—the future minister to breach the halls of the Curia and the future mathematician to earn a few coins and live more comfortably.

Unlike the cardinal, who was always indifferent to religion—he understood that his role in the Church was political, so he never even said mass—the professor's father had left the priesthood in a crisis of faith and raised his children as far as possible from the Catholic hierarchy, in the city of Pisa, where the tolerant breezes of the Most Serene Republic of Venice blew. The cardinal and the mathematician-lutenist kept up the mysterious bond of friendship all their lives, thanks to their habit of playing music together when they met.

When the professor was orphaned, the cardinal took him under his wing, though from afar. By now he was infatuated with the colossal, audacious intelligence of his friend's eldest son, and he supported him beyond the call of friendship during his rise up the steep staircase of academia.

During his stays at the Palazzo Madama, the mathematician did his best to avoid the parade of celebrities who daily visited the salons, the interminable banquets, the musical evenings that began with an appreciation of lutes and ended in lecherous dances; saggy bishops paired with taut-bellied seminarists—boys who, after all, had been wearing skirts since they arrived. Usually he slipped out early and, before returning to his room, went down to the servants' quarters to see whether he might find the painter working or about to go out and set the night on fire with his entourage of outlaws and tarts. The barbarity of these revelries was more pleasing to him.

If the artist was working on a painting, he wouldn't go out, so the mathematician would watch him, intent on copying a single toe of one of his models, who were made to sit for hours by candlelight. These were the professor's favorite Roman nights and the only moments when he could talk to the Lombard in a state of sobriety. When the painter was idle and without commissions, the mathematician also enjoyed his lowlife indulgences. There was a furious sincerity about his nighttime exploits; a rage that later impressed itself on his paintings.

It was at one of the banquets upstairs, when he couldn't escape early, that the professor came upon the most beautiful piece of ecclesiastical attire he would ever see in his life: a miter in iridescent shades that an overseas bishop had sent to one of the popes to be worn at the sessions of the Council of Trent. The miter had been exhibited at the dinner not as a work of art, or as a memento of a moment of schism in the history of the Church of Rome, but as an object of such extreme luxury that it was almost obscene: garb fit for the brothel of an archbishop. Even in this setting, the mathematician found it dazzlingly beautiful because of the way it reflected the candlelight.

The next day he went to examine it at the office of Federico

Borromeo, the cardinal who had brought it. When it was in his hands he realized that the renderings of the divine word and the Crucifixion that adorned it weren't painted on satin, as he had imagined, but were made of feathers; it looked more like a scene stitched in the finest filigree than an oil painting. Where did this come from, he asked the cardinal. From a place called Mechuacán, in the New World, he was told. What artist made it? Some Indians there. He gave it a few turns; he remembered it being shinier. Though the craftsmanship of the thing was astonishing in itself, the night before he'd had the sense that it gave off light, so he was rather disappointed to discover that it had only been a kind of hallucination. Why doesn't it glow as it did last night, he asked, after weighing and smelling it. It's a secret of the Indians; it only shines by candlelight. Despite the cardinal's reluctance, the mathematician managed to borrow it for a few hours to study it with the increasingly powerful lenses that he was developing. He returned it the next day, admitting that he was very impressed.

The professor never wrote a theory of light like the one he completed on the trajectories of bullets—a theory that proved very handy for the artist when it came to making money on the tennis courts of the piazza. He always wished he had written it. In a letter to Piero Dini in 1615 he told him about the iridescent feathers of the New World and a phosphorescent stone that he had acquired at great cost in Padua. After his years in cells, he confessed in another letter, he would be content to live a whole second life of bread, water, and prison bars if he could better develop his scattered ideas on the flow of light.

It's the fucking mathematician, said the duke to the poet when the slaughter of the second game was over. Did you see how he spent the whole first set doing sums? Who knows what he said to him during the changeover; he found the one spot you can't reach. The poet raised his eyebrows: I hadn't noticed, he said.

Te Deum
amid the Ruins

——◆ • ◆——

On February 28, 1525, Shrove Tuesday, the emperor Cuauh-témoc dreamed of a dog. He waited calmly, aided by the chains that bound him to his cot, for Tetlepanquetzal—the lord of Tacuba and his comrade in captivity—to wake so he could tell him. Are you sure, the sleepy-eyed prince asked the emperor, who by now had spent several hours doing nothing but staring at the ceiling of the improvised cell they shared. I'm sure, he answered; the dog sat before me all night, licking my feet. Tetlepanquetzal wiped his mouth with the back of his chained hand. What feet, he asked.

By this Carnival Tuesday morning, the prince had spent one thousand two hundred and seventy-six nights going to sleep in the hope that this bitterest of ill fates would pass from his broken body, maimed and mutilated and in chains, as if chains were necessary.

Since the night when a squad of Tlaxcaltecas had captured him as he tried to leave Mexico City to muster a last stand at one of the ports on Lake Texcoco, Cuauhtémoc had prayed to all his gods every day to bring him death. For reasons that have never been clear, Hernán Cortés decided to keep him alive along with Prince Tetlepanquetzal, who was by his side on the last royal barge afloat on the Lake of Mexico.

The emperor Cuauhtémoc, a young man who had organized the defense of Tenochtitlan the best he could and who had no kin left to inherit the crown, was captured on August 13, 1521, Saint Hippolytus's Day. The news spread immediately through the city, whose defenders simply went out into the streets unarmed, possibly hoping for a drink of fresh water before they were butchered: on the first day of the siege the Spaniards had cut off the water supply, and Lake Texcoco was sulfurous and poisonous. They came out of their houses in a state vacillating between defiance and apathy: they had sworn to their gods that if there was no City of Mexico—"the root of the world"—there would be no Mexicas, so they surrendered themselves to the ritual of being sacked, raped, beheaded, and devoured by dogs, almost happy to go quickly.

There was a muted quality to the fall of Tenochtitlan. Though it caused more planetary aftershocks than the equally monumental falls of Jerusalem and Constantinople, and though in all three cases entire worlds were toppled and swallowed up by the pool of blood and shit that history leaves when it goes mad, in Tenochtitlan everything was filtered through the melancholy of guilt, as if the men who finally got their way were certain that they were breaking something they wouldn't be able to put back together again.

There isn't a trace of gloating in the letter in which Cortés tells the king that the spine of the Aztec empire has finally been broken and its Mexica rulers crushed. It's as if the three months of siege had left him as exhausted and prey to hunger and thirst as those he had defeated. There was no victory ceremony or triumphal procession. A Te Deum was said amid the ruins, and the next day everyone embarked on the tedious task of reconfiguring the smashed city.

The thirteenth of August, 1521, survives in the written record only as a perfunctory accounting of the arrest of Cuauhtémoc, and there would have been no hero in this war—and perhaps no villain either—if not for the fact that when the pillaging Spaniards reached the palace of Moctezuma, it was discovered that it hid no treasure. The gold won in battle wasn't nearly enough to pay the troops who for years had been desperate to get their deserts, and the captain general decided, in the first of his terrible administrative decisions, to keep Cuauhtémoc alive, to use him as a scapegoat, torturing him in the public plaza to make him confess where he was hiding the mountains of gold that clearly didn't exist.

They scalded the emperor's hands and feet with boiling oil. They didn't kill him even though he begged Cortés, politely at first, then in screams, and finally with curses. Bernal Díaz del Castillo—or whoever wrote his testimony—has nothing but pity for the emperor and shame on behalf of his captain in his account.

One thousand two hundred and seventy-six nights after the torture, on Shrove Tuesday, 1525, when an Indian by the name of Cristóbal Mexicaltzingo entered the improvised cell in what is now Campeche to bring the emperor and the lord of Tacuba before Cortés, they were smiling.

Cuauhtémoc was strangled that same morning, in the dark and without trial. A rumor accused him of planning an impossible mutiny of cripples against the conquest expedition of Las Hibueras and El Petén, on which the captain general had dragged him in chains so as not to leave him alone in a Mexico City still under reconstruction.

It's funny in a way that he was killed on Carnival Tuesday: maimed as he was, and in chains, he played the rather obvious part of the ugly king who must die so that the world is submerged in the primal waters of Ash Wednesday and forty days later rises up, saved.

As soon as the prince of Tacuba and the emperor of Mexico had breathed their last stale breaths, Cortés gave the order for their heads to be cut off and displayed in the most visible spot of the town where they had spent their last night, for the edification of anyone who might think it was a good idea to mutiny in the confusion of the jungle. It was the Indian Cristóbal who was charged with severing the heads and mounting them on two spikes driven into a pochota tree. The local cacique didn't protest at this scandalous profaning of the village's sacred tree: he had been doing his best to survive by putting on a convincing show of Christianity ever since an army of starving men had sprung from the woods like a nightmare on the morning of Carnival Monday.

Before Cristóbal set the imperial head on its stake, Cortés asked him to shear it. Make a bundle of the hair and take it to Doña Malinche, he said to the Indian, folding down his sleeves as he sat for breakfast in the cacique's hut. Tell her, he went on, to weave me a scapular that will grant me the protection of God, the Holy Virgin, and Guatemotzin's demons. From around his neck he took a chain with a silver medallion of the Virgin of the town of Guadalupe in Extremadura and gave it to him: Tell her to set this in it.

The rest of the emperor's body was hacked to pieces, burned, and scattered. Cortés had read his Julius Caesar and he didn't want anyone to steal the body of this Vercingetorix that fortune had set in his path. That was why he had him brought to the Términos Lagoon, and that was why he disposed of the body before the most organized southern cities could see any kind of message in it.

He forgot all about the scapular that he had ordered to be made because, liberated of Cuauhtémoc, he turned his back on all his recent past; once begun, he also got rid of Malinche, his translator, political adviser, military strategist, and lover. He ordered one of his men to marry her and take her back to Orizaba. As a wedding gift he gave them the village's communal land and the Indians who worked it, to do with as they pleased.

No Catgut
for Spain

—◆•◆—

Racket. In ball games it is a thick board with which the ball is struck. It is about two spans, with a grip or handle, which grows broader until it ends in a kind of half-moon. It is generally covered in parchment, which is stuck on with glue so that no stroke may score the board.

Diccionario de autoridades, Madrid, 1726

The Second Burning of Rome

—◆•◆—

A portrait that does Pius IV justice would have to be taken at table—a painting of light and shadow in which he presides over a grand Baroque dinner. After all, his papacy was the amuse-bouche of all the pyres of modernity.

In this ideal portrait of Pius IV, he sits with a glass of white wine in one hand and a fistful of almonds in the other. His royal purple soutane is tacky with salt, his beard greasy from the thick slices of wild boar sausage he has eaten. By his side is a small table, upon which rests a china plate with strips of tuna. The pope, food, wine. But there is more: The table is set on a patio. It is nighttime, there are torches; there is an army of servants swaddled in velvet, attentive to the wishes of His Holiness. In the portrait, Pius IV is up in the heights, watching Rome burn— the pyre and modernity, the pyre of modernity making room for itself—and then all Europe, the flames, his face alight. Europe had overheated with the discovery and occupation of the Caribbean, the conquest of Mexico and the subjugation of Peru, the rebellions of the reformist bishops. He, a practical man with no agenda, only contributed the spark that started the blaze when he signed the accords of the Council of Trent into law.

Let's not leave him alone as the inferno licks at his silk slippers. With him, naturally, is Carlo Borromeo, the ideologue and publicist par excellence of the Counter-Reformation, and Montalto, the inquisitor who executed it in blood and fire.

Montalto would rise to the papacy as Sixtus V—a backward name, which is perhaps why he was granted a nickname for the ages: the Iron Pope. Borromeo didn't have the imperial gravitas of his interlocutors, but he was the éminence grise behind Pius IV and Gregory XIII. He died young and was raised to sainthood immediately upon his death. His body is buried under the presbytery of the cathedral of Milan in what is today the Scurolo di San Carlo, in a sarcophagus of rock crystal like Snow White's. His creepy mummified body—a little black masked thing, covered in gems and robes—can still be seen for the price of two euros.

In order for the three cardinals to be gathered in an ideal portrait of Pius IV watching the blaze, a reason must be concocted here. The pope, for example, knowing that Borromeo was away from Milan on a business trip to the Vatican, might have invited him to report on how the city was recovering from the plague. Montalto, attending to practical matters with the pope, might have stayed for dinner with them.

Or it might be Borromeo who had invited the pontiff and the inquisitor to a private conclave at the loggia of the Palazzo Colonna, the official residence of the Milanese nobility in the papal city. A secret, breakaway conclave of three men who, though on different courses, had found common cause at Trent when they articulated the shape of the Baroque century to come. They were brothers-in-arms.

If the meeting were to happen in 1565—when Spain took possession of the Philippines and the world at last became round as a tennis ball—Pius IV, the oldest of the three, would be feeling the call of death in his bones, his Lombard eyes fading from their customary placid blue to the transparent color that allows the passage of visions. This, then, would be the last private meeting of the three men. The pope is sixty-six, his beard white, his breathing labored from the excess weight visited on him by the satisfaction of his wants. Carlo Borromeo is twenty-seven: gaunt, wiry, with the long, poorly shaven face of an El Greco model. Cardinal Montalto, all-powerful inquisitor with too many scores pending, is at the brutal crossroads of forty-five: too old for everything, too young for everything. During the meeting he'll learn that when Pius dies he'll be left out in the cold because he's been working so hard to hang, draw, and quarter half of Europe that he hasn't developed the political relationships in the Roman Curia to survive the papal change of guard.

In this ideal portrait of Pius IV looking out over the conflagration with his brothers-in-arms, the three are in good humor, in a mood to render judgment. They sit on the slope of the Esquiline Hill, in the loggia of the garden of the Palazzo Colonna, watching Rome from the spot where in the sixteenth century the ruins of a Roman temple still stood, the temple from which Nero watched the city burn. The three men are on the terrace, spellbound by the dancing of the flames; servants and guards among the toppled ivy-covered columns, the vegetation exuding its oils in something like a futile last stand against the blaze of the Counter-Reformation, which in the end will lay waste to everything.

Miserliness

◆─•─◆

On March 14, 1618, Quevedo wrote a letter to Pedro Téllez Girón in which he described in minute and cruel detail the greed with which the duke of Uceda, the king's favorite, had received a bribe. Quevedo says that the people at the Palace of Uceda were so miserly and so quick to snatch up any small dispensation that they didn't even return his packing materials: "Even the cotton was not scorned, being used for candlewicks." A use was also found for the boxes in which the gifts came: "The wooden boxes in which everything was packed thought to escape notice, being flawed, but when it was discovered that they were made of poplar, with great celebration they were shared out to be used for tennis rackets."

On Names, and the Troubled History and Politics of How Things Are Named

—◆•◆—

Living in Mexico had become a source of more anxiety than pleasure when I moved to New York. My reason for leaving is still hard to put into words, but it has something to do with a problem of nomenclature.

Back home we stopped calling things by their names long ago, and now, as the serpent heads of our plumed Hydra multiply endlessly, we're left without the spell to counter their poison.

Mexican Spanish, at times so disconcerting and easy to misinterpret, gets its warmth and courtesy from Nahuatl: the gentlest and most gracious of tongues; an airy, birdlike form of speech. When someone from Madrid or Montevideo walks into a room, he says, *"Permiso,"* and that's it. In contrast, a Mexican erects a syntactic edifice so complicated that it requires both a negative clause and a verb in the conditional: "If it's no trouble, might I come in?" If the game recounted in these pages had been played in sixteenth-century Mexico, and if Hernán Cortés had invited the emperor Moctezuma to have it out on the court as Charles V and Henry VIII used to do, they wouldn't have rudely shouted *"Tenez!"* but would have said, "Excuse the service, please."

According to Nahuatl etiquette, the polite way to address a person is with the diminutive *tzin*. The pre-Hispanic name of the Virgin of Guadalupe was Tonantli, or Our Mother, but no one ever called her that, then or now. She was—and still is—Tonantzin, Our Little Mother. In Spanish we refer to her as La Virgen, but when the faithful petition her for something and address her directly, they call her Virgencita. It's not that they're sappier or more sentimental than other Spanish speakers; it's just that Mexican Spanish is crisscrossed with the scars of Nahuatl. In our mental hard drives, the file of the mother tongue still opens at certain prompts, even though it's been two or three hundred years since we spoke it.

It's still hard to believe that during the sixteenth century, there was an enormous empire, governed by an extraordinarily bloodthirsty ruling class, whose prince was addressed as a child: Tizoctzin, Ahuizotzin, Moctezumoctzin. This practice is bizarre and seductive, and I think it's crucial to make note of it, because it's still alive today: the bandit and killer Joaquín Guzmán is called Chapo, or Shorty. No one calls the president by a diminutive anymore, but I'm not sure there has been an incumbent of that office who deserved it either. Maybe a diminutive is something one earns. The only twentieth-century president who was truly loved by the people, Lázaro Cárdenas, was called Tata, "Grandpa" in Nahuatl.

Full disclosure: If you are reading this page, you are reading a translation. In some languages, readers don't flinch as the emperor Cuauhtémoc becomes Cuauhtemoctzin, Guatémuz, or

Guatemotzin, depending on who is speaking to him and in what context. In other languages, the mutating names seem to throw readers into a state of confusion. I'm not sorry about that: a whole vision of the universe would be lost if Malinalli Tenépatl, the Mayan princess who was Hernán Cortés's translator, didn't refer to Cuauhtémoc as Cuauhtemoctzin. Something would also be lost if it weren't recorded that Hernán Cortés—who was either very arrogant or very deaf—called the emperor by the hideous name of Guatémuz, which was what he heard and then set down in his letters to Charles V. I don't know—and it's impossible to know, of course—whether Cortés ever called him Guatemotzin, as he does in this book when he's trying to be diplomatic, but the function of a novel is precisely that: to name what is lost, to replace the void with an imaginary archive.

And it works the other way round too: if Cuauhtémoc had ever spoken to Malinalli, he would have called her Malitzin, as if the political class to which he belonged had not given her up as a sex toy to a local leader just because he won a battle. This means something, and if it went unmentioned, this book would no longer be a machine for understanding the world, or the ways in which we name the world. We know that Malinche was the terrible word Cortés came up with for Malinalli. He could not say, or he didn't want to say, Malitzin. His pronunciation of Nahuatl was so atrocious that it confused people: the Indians who survived the conquest called *him* Malinche; they didn't understand that he was simply trying to address his mistress politely in Aztec terms.

During the conquest, some contest played out between the Mayan princess subjected to the indignity of sexual servitude and Cuauhtémoc, the young emperor witnessing the annihilation of his realm. And this duel, I'm convinced, is visible in the succession of names adopted by the woman whose resentment shifted the balance of the world: Malinalli, princess-whore; Malitzin, mouthpiece of the soldiers and politicians who held history in their fists perhaps without realizing it; Doña Marina (her Catholic name), mother of the conquistador's children and owner of a Spanish palace on the outskirts of Mexico City; Malinche, the bitch who vanished from history after having delivered America to the Europeans. Over the course of her life, Malinalli Tenépatl was many people, like all of us, but she had the privilege of possessing a different name for each incarnation. In today's Spanish, her name is the root of an adjective: *malinchista* means someone who prefers the foreign and disdains his own culture.

Caravaggio's name or lack of a name is so important that Peter Robb, one of his most painstaking biographers, doesn't dare to name him in the book he wrote about him. It is titled *M: The Man Who Became Caravaggio*, because no document exists to prove that as a child he bore the name he claimed as an adult: Michelangelo Merisi. It's a fact that his father's last name was the Milanese Merixio, and that he changed it to the Roman Merisi when he began to sell paintings; it's likely that his name was Michele and when he got to Rome he added the "angelo" to emulate the most famous artist of the day. Later he decided to erase it all and adopt the generic and enigmatic "Caravaggio," the name of his undistinguished and insignificant hometown. It's as if Andy Warhol had signed his serigraphs "Pittsburgh."

Certainly Cuauhtémoc could be simply Cuauhtémoc in this

book, but to dispense with the enigma of the name changes, or to list them at the end of the book and thus create an illusion of clarity where there is none, would be to banish the reader to the stands, to bounce him off the court. A novel isn't a Cartesian diagram. Pope Pius IV's surname was Medici, though he wasn't related to the grand duke of Florence; there were two Borromeos who were bishops of Milan; all of Hernán Cortés's male offspring were called Martín and all of the important women in his life were called Juana. These facts were confusing in their own time, and there's no reason why they shouldn't be confusing in a novel that doesn't aspire to accurately represent that time, but does want to present it as a theory about the world we live in today.

The question here is the responsibility I bear in the face of the reasonable fear that what is being said won't be understood. The risk is worth the weight of that responsibility. The sole duty of a writer is to minister to his readers: to liberate them from inexactitude out of respect for the mysterious and touching pact of loyalty that they make with books. But the problem is that I don't always know why name changes are significant in Mexico, and my hunch is that there is a whole history and politics behind it. When something is clear to a writer, I think it's fair to ask him not to obscure it, but when something is unclear I think it should be left that way. The honest thing is to relay my doubts, and let the conversation move one step forward: the readers may know better.

Judith Beheading Holofernes

—◆—•—◆—

J*udith Beheading Holofernes* measures about four and a half by
six and a half feet. It's a difficult painting to transport, but
not unwieldy enough to warrant asking for help: gripping it by
the lower upright edge and resting the central crosspiece on the
shoulder, one should be able to carry it across the piazza of San
Luigi dei Francesi in Rome. After Caravaggio had painted it, he
did just that: hoisting the painting onto his shoulder in his studio, he crossed the courtyard that separated the service quarters
from the kitchen and walked from one side of the piazza to the
other to deliver it to the mansion of the banker Vincenzo Giustiniani, who wanted it.

It was the last work Caravaggio painted before becoming
Rome's greatest art-world celebrity on the complicated cusp of
the sixteenth century. He must have delivered it before the
church of San Luigi dei Francesi opened its doors for the early
mass; he was scandalously behind on the commission for the
Calling and the *Martyrdom*, which would hang in the church's
Contarelli Chapel. The delivery date on the contract that he
had signed with the congregation of San Luigi dei Francesi had
twice been missed, and he was so late that Cardinal Matthieu

Contarelli, who had planned the chapel in honor of his name-sake apostle, had already died.

There were reasons for Caravaggio's delay: the decoration of the Contarelli Chapel was his first commission for a place of worship and he wanted these two pieces of public art to be masterpieces—as they indisputably are. He also understood that the lucky star lighting his path was powered by the generosity of del Monte and Giustiniani, so he attended to the needs of his patrons before those of his clients.

The morning of August 14, 1599, when Caravaggio carried the painting from the Palazzo Madama to the banker's palace, was surely hot, which means the artist probably wasn't wearing the legendary black cloak in which he appears draped in abso-lutely all the descriptions—and there are many of them—of his arrests in the police precincts of Rome.

Merisi was a man of extremes, a desperate man. Between the summer and autumn of 1599 he had one of his most productive periods, which means he must have been nervously sober when he delivered the painting to the Palazzo Giustiniani—bruised circles under his eyes, dull skin, the glazed look of those who've worked for days on end without rest. Caravaggio didn't draw: he painted directly in oil on canvas; and he didn't trust the prodi-gious Mannerist capacity for imagination: he staged the scenes he painted in his studio, with real models. He did the work all at once, laboring by the millimeter for days on end, using sources of controlled light that he reproduced on the canvas just as they appeared to him.

The scene in which Judith cuts off the head of King Holo-fernes takes place at night, which means that the windows of the studio must have been covered and the models painted by candlelight. Chances are that Caravaggio delivered the piece the moment he decided it was finished. He was in desperate need of money to buy the materials to finally embark on the monumental oils for San Luigi dei Francesi.

He must have crossed the plaza quickly, furtively, without a word to the loiterers who had missed his company during the nights it took him to finish the painting. He must have carried it uncovered, because he couldn't even drape it with a cloth—an oil painting takes years to dry—and neither could he rest the painted surface on his shoulder. Once at the door of the Palazzo Giustiniani he must have lowered it and, propping it on the toes of his boots so that it wasn't soiled by the dirty ground, banged the doorknocker with one hand as he balanced the painting on his feet with the other.

Giustiniani kept huntsman's hours, which means that when Caravaggio arrived he must have been in his office, reviewing the end-of-day accounts from the previous afternoon. Or in the courtyard itself, brushing the manes of his horses before the grooms fed them. He would already have drunk his cup of chocolate, the only luxury he allowed himself. Someone must have been sent to ask him what to do with the madman who was outside with a horrible painting. If Giustiniani was in the courtyard, it would likely have been one of the cooks who reached him with the news: A dreadful sight. The painting or the madman? Both, but especially the painting. Give him something to eat; let him leave the thing in the kitchen. And he must have hurried to the *studiolo* to retrieve from his writing desk the rest of the money he owed the painter. The entry is set down in his books in his own hand: *"Ago 14 / 60 scudi / Pitt Meritzio."* Maybe it was then that he began to turn over the possibility of hanging the painting here, where he would be the only one to see it.

For years it was thought that this eccentric behavior—commissioning a painting in order to be its only viewer—was due to the brutal violence displayed on the canvas: the heroine yanking the tyrant's tangled hair with one hand while with the other she slits his throat like a pig's, his head already twisted and about to come off, the streams of blood, the engorged nipples, the grotesque excitement of the serving woman who holds a cloth to receive the remains when the last tendon is severed. But this doesn't explain the painting's trajectory: at some point Giustiniani gave it—curtains and all—to Ottavio Costa, another Genovese banker, partner in the most substantial of Giustiniani's Vatican investments, and a hunting companion.

There's no record of the transfer of the painting, but it ended up in the collection that Costa left when he died, along with another work originally bought by Giustiniani, painted by Caravaggio and featuring the same woman.

In 1601, the celebrated prostitute Fillide Melandroni, who had served as model for Judith and also for Mary Magdalene in the painting *Martha and Mary Magdalene*, was arrested one night at one of the entrances to the Palazzo Giustiniani; she was in the company of her pimp, Ranuccio Tomassoni.

It's likely that the whore was Giustiniani's lover and that after the scandal of her being arrested at his very door—a tip-off, surely; the vengeance of a lesser moneylender hurt by the banker's large-scale operations—he must have gotten rid of the two paintings in which she appeared.

The loss must also have been hard for Caravaggio: he didn't paint Fillide Melandroni again after this arrest, and she was far and away his most spectacular model: not just a figure of exceptional beauty, but a collaborator with the gift of a unique dramatic sense—she is also Saint Catherine of Alexandria in the monumental work retained by del Monte, which today can be seen in the Thyssen-Bornemisza collection in Madrid.

Incidentally, Ranuccio Tomassoni was the man Caravaggio killed on the Campo Marzio tennis court a few years later. It was a murder long foreshadowed, with both men making frequent visits to the headquarters of the Roman police to report each other or to be arrested following those reports—all stemming from shouting matches and knife brandishings that grew gradually more severe. Surely the nights that Fillide spent at Merisi's studio weren't devoted solely to the glory of art, and their nearness wasn't only professional, on either side: he didn't just paint, and she didn't just sleep with him for money.

At some level, Giustiniani and Caravaggio must have been conscious that they were sharing the same woman—who belonged to Tomassoni. In addition, the banker was a political ally and comrade in intellectual dissidence of Cardinal del Monte, known by all to occasionally offer his monumental cardinal's ass to be buggered by Caravaggio with all the elemental hunger of the painter's years of want. Never were the connections among politics, money, art, and semen so tight or so murky. Or so unashamedly happy, tolerant, and fluid. Giustiniani dispatched his Lombardy boars, Caravaggio dispatched his Venetian cardinal, Fillide dispatched both men. Everyone was happy.

These were also the years when Merisi discovered the chiaroscuro that forever changed the way a canvas can be inhabited: he did away with the foul Mannerist landscapes—the saints, virgins, and great men posing with intelligent gaze on a backdrop of fields, cities, sheep. He shifted the sacred scenes indoors to focus the spectators of his paintings on the humanity of the characters. Fillide was his vehicle for moving the machinery of art a step forward. Not a saint playing a saint, but a woman stripped of superior attributes, and in action; she was a poor woman, as she had to be for the Counter-Reformation credo to make sense. Before Caravaggio, biblical figures were portrayed as millionaires: the richness of their garments was the reflection of spiritual bounty.

An affluent saint in a landscape stands for a world touched by God. A saint in a room stands for humanity in the dark: a humanity distinguished by its ability to continue to believe, in a world in which faith is already impossible; a material humanity smelling of blood and saliva; a humanity that no longer watches from the sidelines, that does things.

Second Set,
Third Game

———◆·◆———

Game. The poet flung his racket on the ground, betraying his desperation for the first time. The artist sprawled on the pavement, his arms outstretched, his smile beatific. Set to the Lombard, cried the mathematician, one–one; tiebreak for the court. Osuna approached the poet. He said into his ear that he had to stop acting like a child and get ready to kick and bite if necessary: If you're not on the service side, you're fucked; when you were on the receiving side you couldn't even get it near the motherfucking dedans.

Ball Game

—◆•◆—

He took the palm-leaf cone. What are they, asked Cortés through Malinche. By now she had learned enough Spanish to interpret directly. Pumpkin seeds roasted in honey, said Cuauhtémoc to Malitzin. The conquistador waited for the Spanish version, took a handful of seeds, and ate them one by one, his eyes on the ball game. They were sitting in the front row, with their legs dangling over the wall, while beneath them the athletes were breaking their backs trying to keep the ball from hitting the ground without touching it with their hands or feet.

During the break before a serve, Cortés showed signs of curiosity—something he did possess, despite his reputation. Which ones represent the underworld and which ones the heavens, he asked Malitzin to inquire. When Cuauhtémoc heard the question—deposited perhaps too close to his ear by the translator—he spat the pumpkin seed shells so that they landed at the very edge of the court. It's Apan against Tepeaca, he said, shrugging his shoulders slightly. Then he got up and went to bet a few cacao beans on Tepeaca.

Hernán Cortés and Cuauhtémoc had met in the infamous

year of 1519, when the visit of the fearsome ambassadors of the
king of Spain to the imperial city of the Mexicas was still a courtesy call. Emperor Moctezuma had tried to dissuade his visitors
from coming to the city of Tenochtitlan by all the means at his
disposal—especially bribery—and they had resisted every temp-
tation, held in check by their captain's promise that the imperial
gold would be theirs as soon as they had conquered the trum-
peted Aztec capital. Moctezuma's grand fuckup—the mistake
that changed the world—was not having killed them when they
first disembarked, before they were of any consequence.

When he had no choice but to welcome the recent arrivals to
his palace, he waited on them with reluctance and fear. It wasn't
superstition that made him afraid of them, as legend has it. He
was terrified because they had arrived at the city gates at the
head of a troop of rebellious nations from all over the empire.
Never in the two hundred years that the Aztecs reigned su-
preme in Mexico had anyone put together an army like the one
that Cortés mustered from the entire east of the realm. None
of the cities loyal to Moctezuma had been able to halt them,
and though the survival instincts of Spaniards and Aztecs—the
two minority groups in the contest—made it necessary for one
side to say that they hadn't come to conquer anything and for
the other side to believe them, everyone knew—regardless of
how hard they tried to pretend otherwise—that sooner or later
the ground beneath their feet would become a mire watered
with the thick broth of slaughter.

Cortés and Moctezuma met at the end of the Tacuba causeway, where the church of Jesús Nazareno stands today, at the
intersection of República del Salvador and Pino Suárez. The

tlatoani gave the captain a necklace of jade beads and received a pearl necklace in exchange—probably strung by Malitzin. The two of them walked to the royal palace, whose foundations today lie under the Palacio Nacional. The visit, though ominous, wasn't directly catastrophic: Cortés had presented himself in Tenochtitlan with his Spanish company alone, to avoid the awkwardness of being seen surrounded by sworn enemies of the Aztecs. The emperor was accompanied by the kings of the Triple Alliance, the caciques of all the lakeside estates and their captains, among whom was Cuauhtemoctzin, a cousin of Moctezuma on his wife's side.

Once they had reached the palace, the full imperial court settled around a courtyard to witness the conversation between Moctezuma and Cortés. It was a conversation in which no one would have understood anything, not only because there could not have been two people in the world more utterly remote from each other, but because what was said in Nahuatl had to be translated first into Chontal and then into Spanish and what was said in Spanish had to be translated first into Chontal and then Nahuatl, since the conquistador didn't trust any tongue but that of Malitzin, who spoke Chontal and Nahuatl, and that of the priest Jerónimo de Aguilar, who spoke Chontal and Spanish.

They exchanged more gifts and messages of goodwill. When they were done, the emperor returned to his sacred routine, removing himself from view of his guests and subjects—no one would see him again until the day of his death—to concentrate on ruling an empire that by this point had shrunk by nearly half.

Over the next eighteen months this empire, already slim,

would grow even slimmer, until it occupied only the Valley of Mexico, and then only Lake Texcoco, and at last only the island city of Tenochtitlan. On August 13, 1521, the empire was nothing but the royal barge, on which Cuauhtémoc was seized trying to escape by water from the wrecked Aztec capital. For once, history was just: a particularly bloody realm reduced to a single barge. Though that didn't mean the good guys had won. The good guys never win.

Several months after his meeting with the Spanish captain, Moctezuma sent word to Cuauhtemoctzin: now that the Spaniards had recovered from the shock of seeing the biggest and most hectic city in the world, he should take Cortés for a stroll, show him something, anything. Get close to him, the blind eunuch messenger whispered to the emperor's cousin; listen to him, let him feel that you're interested in him. Why me, asked Cuauhtémoc. Because you speak Chontal, said the messenger.

The young man had so far been an invincible captain and an intelligent ally of the throne. He was discreet, solitary, trustworthy. Noted for his discipline in a world where discipline was paramount. Tell the emperor I'll take him to the ball game, he replied.

He waited a few days to approach Malitzin, Cortés's Chontal tongue; he waited for the end of the first harvest, which was celebrated with games that were anticipated all year and that were definitely a sight for a foreigner to see.

The Next World

◆—•—◆

The German historian and cultural critic Heiner Gillmeister believes he has discovered the oldest play-by-play account of tennis as we know it. An ur–ball game that predates everything: Italian *calcio*, English cricket, what in French is called *jeu de paume* and in Spanish *pelota*.

The first recorded tennis match in human history took place in hell and was a doubles match. It was played by four demons, using the soul of a French seminarist by the name of Pierre. In time, Pierre became abbot of the monastery of Marienstatt as Petrus I, and found fame. His story was preserved because Caesarius of Heisterbach recorded it in a volume called *Dialogus miraculorum*.

As the story tells it, Pierre the Idiot—as the first tennis player of all time seems to have been known in his youth—made a Faustian stumble. He had a terrible memory and was incapable of concentrating on anything, so to pass his exams at seminary he accepted a gift from Satan. It was a stone that contained all the knowledge of man, and all one had to do to possess that knowledge was squeeze it in one's fist.

Brother Pierre did what any of us might have done in his

place, and he got top marks in his exams without having to study. But one day he fell into something that we would now identify as a comatose state—which in his time was simply death. As he told it later, a foursome of demons extracted his soul from his body, feeling free to play tennis with it since the Idiot had unwittingly accepted the deal when he squeezed the stone.

The four demons, like four ordinary friends, made their way back to hell with the object they had borrowed from the world of the living and played a tennis match with their metaphysical ball. Pierre remained conscious and felt the satanic serves and returns in his flesh. According to his testimony, the match was particularly torturous because—as everyone knows—demons have steel fingernails and never trim them.

The fact that the first written account of a tennis game describes an eschatological battle recounted from the perspective of someone called Petrus I, pope of an alternative church of condemned men and killers, a church of ball and racket, is one of the little bones that history occasionally throws us.

In the second part of *Don Quixote*, Altisidora has a vision, in which she sees devils playing with rackets of fire, using books "full of wind and stuffing" as balls. Unlike *Don Quixote*, these books are in no condition to survive a second round. After the first volley "there wasn't one ball that could withstand another or was in any condition to be served again, and so books old and new came in quick succession."

In hell, souls are balls and bad books are balls. Demons play with them.

Art

◆ · ◆

It's said that Caravaggio's dagger had a Latin inscription carved on both sides of its blade. It read *"Nec spe"* on one side and *"Nec metu"* on the other: "Without hope. Without fear."

Regarding Most
Popes' Utter Lack of
a Sense of Humor

◆—•—◆

In the print collection of the Metropolitan Museum of Art there is a lithograph by an anonymous Flemish artist dating from about 1550. On the front it reads *"Palazzo Colonna,"* and on the back *"La Loggia dei colonnesi con la Torre Mesa edificate tra le rovine del Tempio di Serapide."* The Colonnas had long been an all-powerful family, and the museum in the Italian capital that still bears their name gives a clear idea of the power and wealth they accumulated.

But Rome wasn't always Rome. Or rather: The Rome of Pius IV wasn't the grandiloquent city that Cardinal Montalto rebuilt when he became pope. The Rome of the sixteenth century, village-like and scattered, is best described by Montaigne, who found it so timid and empty that his disappointment became a cliché of Baroque disenchantment. The city was clotted with old and new ruins, among which animals strolled more freely than people. Said the French poet Joachim du Bellay about mid-sixteenth-century Rome:

You seek Rome in Rome, o pilgrim!
and in Rome itself you cannot find Rome.

In the year 1565, when Borromeo, Montalto, and Pius IV might have been drinking a glass of wine as fire rained down on the navel of Catholicism, the Palazzo Colonna wasn't the meringue-trimmed palace it later became. The loggia was a house of red brick, constructed from the remains of the Tempio di Serapide, of which a stretch of frontispiece still stood. It had two floors, five windows, two doors, and a tile-roofed terrace. Behind it, the ruins: the loggia literally leaned against the ancient temple, and around it shrubs, palms, and a group of glade-like trees grew up from the ground and also the walls.

It would be on this cool, modest brick terrace that the cardinals would be sitting as if in a box at the theater.

Watching the whole world go up in flames, Pius wouldn't sing of the sack of Troy, as Nero did. He would be silent, listening with eyes shut to a snatch of music—the last bit of melody from a time before the universal conflagration that today we casually call "the Baroque"—rocking slightly from side to side, his eyes closed, the hand holding the almonds marking time for an orchestra.

During a pause in the music, he would open his eyes and say to Cardinal Montalto: I have a gift for you. There are other things he could say—for example, what the Argentine writer Leónidas Lamborghini says about the era dawning before the arbiters of Trent: "We have bought Torture instead of Compassion. Fear instead of Mercy. Hate instead of Love. Death instead of Life." Or he could say what he had confessed a few years earlier to his friend Tolomeo Gallio, in a letter in which he reported how troubled he was by the Curia's harassment of Michelangelo and how it had paralyzed him for some time:

"I'm terrified to admit it, but I love his *Last Judgment*. It's a mortal sin, and I'm the Pope!"

Pius IV had watered the little pot in which he planned for Borromeo to blossom, and instead of a plant, a wild boar had grown.

This has to be seen as a film. The pope cuts another slice of sausage and closes his eyes. He opens them and eats.

PIUS IV:
(still chewing)
I have a gift for you, Montalto. It's a modest gift.

The pope waves one hand in the air, the sleeves of the papal robes like a flag. His chamber attendant approaches with a little wooden box trimmed with silver.

MONTALTO:
(smiling)
I'm not a man for jewels.

PIUS IV:
I'm sixty-six years old, no one thought I'd make it to pope but I did; I met Michelangelo and Raphael, Charles V and Francis I were my friends; I invented Carlo Borromeo, here present.

He indicates him with a nod and a raising of eyebrows, part ironic and part grateful.

PIUS IV (CONT.):

Do you think that at this final meeting, our last banquet, I'd give you a mere jewelry box?

The servant brings the gift to the cardinal, who opens it.

MONTALTO:
(taking something out of the chest)
A tennis ball.

He looks at it, holds it up so Borromeo can see it.

MONTALTO (CONT.):
A bit unraveled.

PIUS IV:

That's because it was made from the hair of Anne Boleyn.

MONTALTO:

Who?

PIUS IV:

One of the wives of Henry VIII of England. You missed that particular scandal.

MONTALTO:

Indeed.

PIUS IV:

Put it to good use.

MONTALTO:

The scandal?

PIUS IV:

The ball.

MONTALTO:

I don't play *pallacorda*.

PIUS IV:

Play it. When King Charles and I die, there will be no one to curb France. If you stick your neck out, you'll be stripped of your privileges or skinned alive and quartered, depending on who is left as inquisitor.

The pope looks at Borromeo.

PIUS IV (CONT.):

Or am I mistaken, Carlo?

BORROMEO:

Your Holiness has never been mistaken in politics.

Cardinal Montalto ignores him and looks the pope in the eye.

MONTALTO:

Are you giving me an order?

PIUS IV:

I'm giving you a piece of advice.

There is a silence that both of them fill by turning to look at Borromeo. Though the bishop of Milan is almost twenty years younger than Montalto, the rigors of a life genuinely spent in imitation of Christ's darkest hours have left traces of the rasp of hunger and sleeplessness, and also small tics that make him look like a piece of unedited footage. His cheek twitches, his head jerks, he squeezes the hands that he keeps clasped in his lap, as if to prevent them from escaping in search of something that might prove tasty.

Borromeo gives the pope and the inquisitor-general an affected sidelong glance, his left eyelid blinking shut every so often.

BORROMEO:
(to Montalto)
Let's see, toss me the ball.

He catches the ball thrown by Montalto, his eyes on the pope.

BORROMEO (CONT.):

It's good advice.

PIUS IV:

Will you protect Montalto from the wolves?

BORROMEO:

I'll protect him so long as he protects himself.

He smells the ball.

BORROMEO (CONT.):

So long as he learns to wait while playing tennis
at his palace.

Cardinal Montalto spent nineteen years and two popes in retreat from public life, busily going through the fortune he had amassed by bleeding the enemies of the Counter-Reformation. In his spare time, as if somehow compelled by the passions unleashed in him by architecture, Montalto also spent those years planning how the city would look if it really was the center of the world—a plan he executed with violence and perfectionism once he was named Pope Sixtus V. He invented urbanism, though his name wasn't Urban. It goes without saying that he never played *pallacorda*. The fact that no subsequent pope was called Sixtus after Montalto, who was the fifth, is proof that the Catholic Church is an institution without a sense of humor. But this isn't part of the film. Back to the script.

*Borromeo tosses back the ball. Montalto puts it away in its box
and the pope beckons again.*

PIUS IV:

I have a present for you too, Carlo.

A servant approaches with a brightly colored headpiece.

BORROMEO:

A miter?

PIUS IV:

It's Mexican.

The cardinal furrows his brow.

PIUS IV (CONT.):

It was sent to me by a bishop there. It isn't painted, it's made of feathers: look, it's a little masterpiece.

The servant holds it out to the cardinal and he takes it, disdainfully.

BORROMEO:
(ironically)
Such intricate handiwork, Your Holiness.

He sets it on his knees.

PIUS IV:

May it help you to remember that France isn't
the whole world, that there are many lands and
many souls.

The cardinal sits watching him, making a show of patience.

PIUS IV (CONT.):

Look at it! If you hold it up to the light in just
the right way, it glows.

Borromeo tilts his head, turns the thing.

PIUS IV (CONT.):

Lift it a little.

*When it's just above his head, the colored feathers of the miter
blaze as if struck by a bolt of lightning. Borromeo drops it, and
it falls into his lap. The pope laughs.*

PIUS IV (CONT.):

What did I tell you?

BORROMEO:

Mexico: the Devil's haunt.

PIUS IV:

It's the work of Christian Indians.

BORROMEO:

What am I supposed to do with it?

PIUS IV:

Say Easter mass in it.

BORROMEO:

Why?

PIUS IV:

Because after the dark always comes the light.

BORROMEO:

I know that.

PIUS IV:

No one would guess it.

The pope cut another slice of sausage and closed his eyes as he chewed, thinking that even when Nero burned Rome the fuel ran out eventually, and the two-thirds of the city left waste was rebuilt magnificently. He could almost smell the blanket of ashes that Trent would leave at his feet. He could see how, in the end, once everything was over, a new tree would spring up from the field of ashes, embryonic and amber-hued; a tree of sinew and muscle, its first limb reaching up through the earth; a tree that—once the smoke from the blaze had cleared—would spread its fingers in the sun like a butterfly of flesh. The butterfly's fingernails would be dirty.

Light to the Living
and Lessons
from the Dead

—◆•◆—

ACCOUNT NUMBER 168.

Once again, a dead man appeared to me, calling me
by name, saying that he hadn't come to frighten me,
but to ask me to commend him to God, that he was
Don N, doing penance in Purgatory. In his hand he
carried a ball of fire, and his dry tongue protruded
from his mouth. I asked: Why are you there? He answered: For the sins of ball-playing and partaking of
cold refreshment. He made a reverence to the cross
and disappeared, saying: Jesus be with you.

JUAN DE PALAFOX Y MENDOZA,
Archbishop and Viceroy of New Spain, 1661

Fear

◆ • ◆

By the time Cortés and Cuauhtémoc met, the Spaniards were more than familiar with Tenochtitlan and had been thoroughly observed by half the city, out on walks that exposed their vulnerability. The Mexica people asked themselves, in ever more insistent tones, why Moctezuma didn't surround these interlopers and kill them once and for all. It would be interesting if history had taken a turn in that direction. From a contemporary perspective, Cortés and his company would be like those lesser martyrs who made the miscalculation of going to preach the gospel in Japan.

There would have been a Saint Hernán of Medellín and a Saint Bernal of Medina del Campo. Velázquez would have painted an altarpiece in which their heads appeared at the foot of the temple of Tezcatlipoca, and Caravaggio another called *The Martyrdom of Saint Jerome of Aguilar*: a canvas that captured Cortés's translator's terror just before his tongue was cut out. Beside him, covering her mouth, one of Merisi's tarts would have played an approximate green-eyed Malitzin. It would be a chiaroscuro set in small-town Rome, remote and squalid, as

Europe always was and would have continued to be if not for the flow of American ore.

Malitzin told Cortés that Cuauhtémoc had approached her. They had just been making love, as so many cheesy writers would have it, though for La Malinche and the captain—scarcely equipped for such a thing—it was more like the scuffling of two blind children.

The conquistador panted, lying on his belly on the cotton pallet as the Mayan princess turned translator, now lubricated with semen, dug about in her pubic hair in the hope of giving herself the satisfaction her man hadn't provided. I saw Cuauhtemoctzin in the market today, she said, kneading the clitoris that changed the world. By now, Doña Marina was the only one of Cortés's associates who could go out into the city without being escorted by an armed company. She was also, at least in Cortés's not inconsiderable experience, the only woman who could do politics and masturbate at the same time.

The captain moved next to her and sniffed her armpit. He squeezed the hand that she was touching herself with, without preventing its circular motion. Who is that, he asked. Moctezuma's favorite captain. And why does it make you so hot that this captain wants to talk to me? Still touching herself, she said: Because men who do it with men turn me on. She closed her eyes. Cortés let her continue. Before burrowing entirely into her own pleasure, she added: He said that he wanted to take you to the ball game tomorrow. Then, in order to come, she found her way to a world in which men weren't animals.

He waited for her to finish, tugging at his beard. When he sensed that she was back, he asked: Do you think it's to kill me?

Her breathing was still ragged when she answered no, that he was a decent sort. Though she had stopped feeling her sex, she protected it with her hand: she hadn't finished; she was resting. The emperor doesn't understand why we haven't left, and he thinks that if someone makes an effort to talk to you, maybe you'll explain. Cortés lifted her hand with what he imagined was delicacy and blew on her. She shivered. Should we believe him? Cuauhtemoctzin is to be believed—he has no flaws, he's a hero, a fanatic; everyone knows that sooner or later he'll be emperor, even he knows it. Cortés made a gesture of unease, indicating that he wasn't convinced by Malinche's confidence. He returned her hand to her sex. She scratched her pubic hair. She said: The truth is that I asked him to kill you; if Moctezuma can't bring himself to do it, sooner or later the people will rise up and *nos van a xingar a todos*, we'll all be fucked, not just you, the only one who thinks it's a good idea for us to stay here and do nothing. We're reconnoitering the plaza, Cortés explained in the bureaucratic tone he had used many times to tell his men why he was subjecting them to a risk they all found unnecessary, but he realized that Malitzin was already off again. With her head thrown back, the translator was imagining Cuauhtémoc— so smooth and hairless—sodomizing the conquistador. He smelled her neck, let her come, and when she had finished climbed on top of her. She asked him to bite her breasts. He loved them, so dark and erect. She came again. He didn't. Collapsed on Malinche, he asked: Should I go? You can't not go; it's Cuauhtemoctzin, he gives the orders; he said he would be there early because it will be crowded. We'll have to tell the troops. He wants us to come alone. He'll betray us. He's a man of his word. I am too, said Cortés, and raising himself on his arms and the tips of his toes, he left a space for her to turn over to offer him her ass. Your people don't know what it means to give your word, she said, squeezing his cock between the hemispheres of her buttocks. When he felt that he had recovered his full erection he lifted her up by the hips and thrust into her without ceremony. She whimpered. A talk, captain to captain, he said as he drove down. She turned her face so that she could see his eyes when she said: You aren't a captain like him. The Spaniard thrust deeper, and pulled her violently by the hair, murmuring in her ear: I'm better. *Ay guapo,* she said between gasps; he isn't a peasant who got lucky.

Cortés's mood deflated too and he rolled back onto the pallet. Acknowledging that he had lost, he turned on his side. He pulled the cotton blanket up from the foot of the cot and covered himself with it, curling into a ball. Don't be a coward, she said; he's a killing machine, but only in combat; with us, he'll be a prince. The Spaniard said nothing. He was listening with all his senses alert to the faintest hint of betrayal in her voice. And you'll like the game, it's fun, and all the lords of the city come with their wives. It was only now that Cortés realized that Malitzin, who had been a princess first and then a slave, and was now something in between, simply wanted to be seen in public in casual conversation with the emperor-to-be. All right, Your Highness, he said; I'll go to the game with Guatémuz, but you can only come if you do what I taught you.

When the princess opened her eyes the next morning, her lover was no longer in bed. He had gone to wake a group of his men to follow them at a prudent distance. I think our next out-

ing should be as a company, on horseback, hightailing it out
of here for the Tacuba causeway, said one of his soldiers, who
was also named Hernando, which meant that everyone called
him by the name of the town he came from—Persona; I don't
think we'll be able to leave on foot without being killed. As
Hernando de Persona spoke, he watched Cortés nervously. No
one will make trouble if they see that I'm with Guatémuz, answered the captain; he's Moctezuma's favorite. How do you
know that? Everyone knows it. The men exchanged doubtful
glances.

By the time the future emperor came for them, Malitzin had
informed her lover that Cuauhtémoc had commanded his first
battle at sixteen and since then he hadn't lost a single one; that
during the five years he'd spent at military college he hadn't
spoken once to anyone; that he didn't eat game, fish, or fowl,
but on feast days he ate the raw flesh of sacrifice victims. This
enumeration of his virtues made her flush. A fucking gem, replied Cortés as he rummaged in his travel bag for something to
wear that had no holes, or that had them only where they could
be hidden under the breastplate and gauntlets of his armor.

Even so, when Cuauhtémoc arrived, he liked him: he was
almost a boy. He wasn't exquisite like the dazzling priests who
passed through the courtyards on their way to rites at the temples, or dressed up like an animal like the other soldiers of his
rank. He was wearing a white shirt and bloomers, a discreet
cloak. No trappings in his hair, which was gathered in a bunch
on top of his head. He wasn't carrying a dagger. Cortés felt
more stifled than ever by the embrace of his armor, the weight
of the grotesque Spanish broadsword on his belt, but he still

believed that suiting up in iron made an impression on the Mexicans. They, of course, thought he must be an utter fool to walk out in the lethal altiplano sun with that massive contrivance on him.

They walked straight for the quay, in the opposite direction of the snaking walls of the sacred city. The ball court is the other way, said Cortés nervously. Through Malitzin, Cuauhtémoc explained that they were going to a much smaller court, in Tlatelolco. Partly to make conversation and also to judge whether this was true, the captain confessed that the Tenochtitlan court had seemed too large ever since they had visited it early on, the walls too far apart and the ring too high. We don't play there, said the Aztec, we stage performances of the first game; no one could lift the ball that high with his hip. It's like a play, explained Malitzin. Cuauhtémoc himself pulled on the rope of the royal barge to bring it closer to her foot.

The Calling of
Saint Matthew

———•———

On September 17, 1599, Caravaggio finished *The Martyrdom of Saint Matthew*. He brought the painting—a pure vortex of senseless violence and repentance—to the sacristy of San Luigi dei Francesi and then set a date for delivery of the second of the three paintings that would be hung in the chapel of the patron saint of accountants and tax collectors: the twenty-eighth of that same month. Since the delivery of the second painting would mean the possibility of finally dedicating the chapel—consecrating it, inviting the pope to the first service in affirmation of his impartiality in the eternal conflict between Spain and France—Caravaggio signed an addendum to the contract in blood, guaranteeing that this time he really would deliver promptly. In exchange for *The Calling of Saint Matthew*, he would be paid the second fifty scudi of the hundred and fifty—a fortune—that he would earn for the complete furnishing of the chapel when he had delivered the third painting, for which he would be allotted more time.

According to legend, Caravaggio didn't sleep for the eleven days it took him to finish the painting, which he certainly hadn't begun before he signed the addendum. The models didn't sleep either. The ones who have been identified are Silvano Vicenti, knife sharpener; Prospero Orsi, soldier; Onorio Bagnasco, beggar; Amerigo Sarzana, arse-fanner; and Ignazio Baldementi, tattooist. Though Caravaggio had the taste to use unknown men as the models for Jesus of Nazareth and Saint Peter, a serious fuss was made because the other actors in the sacred drama were petty criminals and loafers who spent their days loitering around the tennis courts of Piazza Navona. But nothing came of it, beyond the rumors that circulated about the ire of the French clergymen. The paintings were simply magnificent, the pope had already been summoned for the consecration of the chapel, and the artist was still under the ironclad protection of Cardinal del Monte and Giustiniani.

The third painting, which he delivered much later and which was called *Saint Matthew and the Angel*, would be judged intolerable by the clergymen: in it, the saint is presented as a befuddled beggar; an angel guides the hand with which he writes the Scripture. It was returned. This was the first of many rejections that Caravaggio would receive for painting whatever he felt like painting and not what was expected of him by his patrons and the city's enlightened circles. He had to redo it and was spared further trouble only because Giustiniani bought the painting spurned by the French Congregation. His *Saint Matthew and the Angel* was the best painting in a triptych of masterpieces, and the crown jewel of Giustiniani's collection. Today it can be seen only in photographic form: it was in the Kaiser Friedrich Museum in Berlin when it was bombed by the Allies in 1945.

The Calling of Saint Matthew measures one hundred and twenty-seven inches by one hundred and thirty inches. It's a nearly square painting that—like the *Martyrdom* and *Saint Matthew and the Angel*—should really have been a fresco, but since Caravaggio was an artist with a method and his method required a dark room, controlled sources of light, and models who acted the scene instead of just posing, he had his way.

The artist couldn't have crossed the piazza carrying this painting himself, since the thing was essentially a wall, but because the delivery meant the onset of celebrations for the consecration of the chapel, it must have been a procession full of pomp and circumstance, befitting the artist's irritating conception of courtesy—if his barely controlled cutthroat ways could be called courteous.

One has to imagine Caravaggio exiting his studio in the early-morning hours, after eleven sleepless nights cooped up with seven half-civilized men. The rings under his eyes, the stench, the clenched jaw of someone nearly out of his mind from exhaustion, the impatience with which he must have knocked at the door of the sacristy to ask what time he should deliver the painting.

The Calling of Saint Matthew has all of what would become the artist's signature elements, and it was by far the most revolutionary work of art seen in a Roman place of worship since the inauguration of the Sistine Chapel. Caravaggio paid eloquent testament to Michelangelo's fresco, which he knew well: the hand with which Jesus of Nazareth points to the tax collector quotes the one with which God almost touches the Son of Man in the upper reaches of the Vatican.

As in nearly all of Caravaggio's subsequent sacred paintings, most of the surface of the *Calling* is empty, a dark room whose

black walls—plainly those of his studio—are scarcely inter-
rupted by a window with darkened panes. The single source of
light isn't visible in the painting: it's a skylight, open just a crack
above the actors' heads. Peter and the Messiah, almost in
shadow, point to the tax collector, who gazes at them in surprise
in the company of four sumptuously dressed cronies busy counting coins with sinful concentration. The attire of Jesus and his
fisherman is traditional: biblical robes. But the money changers
look just like Giustiniani's moneylenders and are sitting as they
must have sat on the lower level of his palace, open to clients of
the money-changing tables.

Caravaggio, who was not a modest man, must have
announced—still seized by the fierce exhilaration of someone
who's solved a riddle—that what he was about to deliver was his
best painting to date, better than *Saint Catherine of Alexandria*, accosting a sacristan in breeches with flattened hair. It
must have been agreed that he would bring the painting at midday, when the full flock of French clergymen—and not just
the half-addled old man who said the early mass—would be
present in their beribboned finest.

Maybe it was the two youngest actors in the painting—
Baldementi, the tattooist, and Sarzana, the arse-fanner—who
hoisted up *The Calling of Saint Matthew* in the studio, crossed
the courtyard, and, instead of going through the kitchen or
scullery door as usual, carried it out by the main door, following
the tyrannical instructions of a frenetic Caravaggio. Surely the
rest of the actors in the painting were waiting outside, still
dressed in character. The arse-fanner and the tattooist would
have crossed the piazza, by now crammed with parishioners

and tradesmen, to the cheers of those perhaps moved by the thought that what was happening was truly important—which it was, though they couldn't have known it, since the future has no place in memory. The artist must have gone before them, parting the waters, puffed up with pride. Prospero Orsi, the soldier, was the uninhibited type, ill-equipped to resist fatuity and borrowed glory. Surely at some point in the crossing of the piazza he would have ordered his fellow actors to stop, and demanded that they stage the scene again in front of the painting itself.

The people at the doors of the church—the sacristan, the acolytes, the priests—must have watched the painting go by in as much of a fright as those seeing a movie projected on a wall for the first time, or with the slack-jawed fascination with which my son and I witnessed the early rollout of a high-definition television in an electronics store. The painting must have been propped against the altar as the carpenters prepared to mount it on the wall. The priests must have been uneasy—before they began to be vexed—at the presence of the boy they had so often seen wipe the shit from his little nose in the latrines of the house of the French Congregation, who was now inside the parish twice over, in the painting and in the flesh, and in banker's attire. But this is only conjecture: specialists in the material culture of the seventeenth century continue to debate what exactly an *asciugaculi* did. Pay the gentleman so that they'll leave, the cardinal of Sancy must have said nervously to the sacristan.

The Chase

—◆•◆—

The duke put the ball on the chalk mark that the professor had made, in the first game, on the paving stones of the court after the ball's first bounce off the post. The mathematician certified that it was the right spot and together they proceeded to ceremoniously take down the cord that divided the serving from the receiving court. They bundled it up and gave it to Mary Magdalene, who had requested it from the gallery. Then they took their places opposite where they had set the ball, outside the bounds of the court on either side. The mathematician stood there almost absentmindedly, his hands clasped behind his back. He was so calm that it was a miracle he didn't whistle a Paduan ditty. The duke crouched opposite him, staring seriously at the ball and stroking his beard with his left hand. He exchanged looks with Barral, who put a frankly irresponsible quantity of coins on the line where bets were placed. The other gamblers found seats in the gallery after setting their money on the side of the player they thought would win the race for the serve. Opinions were divided for the first time in the match. Both seconds turned toward the players, who were standing together on the far side of the baseline and jostling shoulders, trying to knock each other off balance even before the start of the race. The duke deferred to the professor. *Eccola!* he shouted, and almost immediately: *Gioco!*

The start of the race might have been disastrous for the artist: his rival used his short leg to hook him by the ankle at the first stride. The trick worked, but the Italian managed to grab the Spaniard by the shirt and pull him down too. They tangled. Blows with the hands were forbidden by the rules, but they kneed each other as many times as they could in the process of freeing themselves.

The artist tried to roll over to make room to get up, but the poet was coiled like a spring, and from where he lay he hurled himself onto the Lombard's back, squeezing his buttocks between his thighs and succeeding in holding him down. From this dominant position he rose, one knee planted in his opponent's back at the height of the kidneys. He levered himself up with a hand flat on the artist's head. Mary Magdalene covered her eyes when she saw how her lover's skull bounced on the pavement. If not for the shouting, the crack would have been audible.

Alone on his feet, the poet rushed for the ball and managed to seize it. But he didn't have time to run and put it in the dedans. The artist, one of his cheeks cut and bleeding, hurled himself full-force at the base of the poet's spine, and both of them fell to the ground again. The Spaniard didn't let go of the ball, but when he tried to get up, he felt the artist's claw on his ankle, pulling him down. He went down again. The painter was on top of him, kneeling on his chest and trying to take the ball away.

Bites, elbow jabs, and clutches followed as both men rolled on the stones like children. At some point the poet ended up on his knees in front of the artist, the ball still firmly in his hand. The Lombard thrust his pelvis into his opponent's face to block his view of the dedans and the Spaniard threw for it with all his soul. The ball went in. The duke cried: Service side.

The spectators returned to the gallery. The mathematician gathered up the coins that the Italians had set on the line. He counted them and crossed the field of battle to hand them over to Barral, who divided them among those who had bet on the Spaniard. He had to leap over the sprawled bodies of both contestants to reach the gallery.

The two players lay side by side, gauging the damage, unable to muster the strength to rise. They were on their backs. More scandalous than the quantity of bruises and scrapes on both was the fact that jutting from their codpieces were such generous erections that they seemed to lift them up. Delightful, said Mary Magdalene, imagining a luscious threesome with pinches, scrapes, and scabs.

Ball

—◆ • ◆—

The ball court, painted with lime on the turf, was divided in half, and each half was divided into four smaller parts. A player was assigned to each quadrant and couldn't leave it. Points were scored by passing the rubber ball through a big wooden ring fixed to the wall. If the ball touched the ground, the team that hadn't made the error won the serve and could shoot for the ring on the first throw. The players rotated and changed court whenever one of the teams had lost the serve thirteen times.

The match was exciting. Apan won. Cortés collected a sum—a dizzying sum, even—from the other gamblers. The Spaniards who had followed him, convinced that they were passing unnoticed as they shrank in their glaring, noisy suits of armor, had watched the match from the opposite side of the trench with no one paying them the slightest attention: if their boss was with Captain Cuauhtémoc, they could do as they pleased. They thought that at last they had been accepted, even commenting among themselves that they should come to see matches more often.

Walking back to the quay, Cortés felt secure enough to ask

the prince why he wasn't taking the opportunity to kill him. My men are far behind, he said; and there are so few of them that the people could easily subdue them. It was the emperor's request, the prince replied, whispering into Malitzin's ear. Not to kill me? To talk, make friends; to see whether you would explain why you haven't left. To the Indian, Malitzin said: I've already explained why you spare him, but he doesn't believe me, and she translated for the Spaniard. Then she asked the future emperor *motu proprio*: Would you have killed him? So fast that he'd be picking up his own head. You don't have a dagger. That's never stopped me, he said, and he explained how a hasty sacrifice to the gods was made on the battlefield: You put the fingers of both hands into the enemy's mouth, you pull on his teeth in both directions until his jaw snaps, then you break his spine with your knee and yank off his head. She felt a tingling between her legs and the urge to have her breasts touched. He was still staring at her impassively; what he had described was exactly what he would have done. What's happening, asked Cortés. She told him. He wasn't amused.

When they reached the outer courtyard of the palace, crammed with bureaucrats hearing the rather vociferous complaints of the inhabitants of the realm, Cortés returned the cacao beans that Cuauhtémoc had loaned him to bet with. Thank him, he said to Malitzin; not for these, but for having kept his word. The Indian looked at him indifferently and answered: Tell him that sooner or later we will face each other in battle, and then I won't let him go. And yet I will spare his life, answered Cortés, but Malinche didn't translate.

Six years later, on Shrove Tuesday, 1525, when Cortés gave the

Indian Cristóbal the order to garrote the emperor in chains, everything had gone so wrong and everyone had changed court so many times that Malitzin was called Marina and it was Cortés who was called Malinche. By now everyone spoke everyone else's languages, and without realizing it they had established a third nation, blind to its own beauty, that no one has ever been able to understand. May your God never forgive you, Malinche, said Cuauhtémoc—now in Spanish—to the conquistador by way of farewell. Don't curse me, replied the captain in Nahuatl; I let you live when your empire was reduced to a barge. I don't curse you for my death, said the emperor, but for all the other deaths; in this land no one will speak your name without shame. Very likely the four thousand masses that Cortés ordered to be said for the repose of his soul were conceived at that instant.

When I myself visited the convent of the Irish sisters in Castilleja de la Cuesta, I asked the mother superior about the ghost of the conquistador. We've never seen him, she said in all seriousness; though there were mothers in the past whom he tried to engage in fornication. And she continued: What he did leave us is a lot of dead people we can't understand, because they speak a language from somewhere else. There's a very handsome one, she said, who can't walk; he has a funny ponytail, on top of his head instead of at the back. Does he make trouble, I asked. He's sitting in that chair, she said.

Treasury of the Castilian or Spanish Language

———— • ————

Ball, or Pelota. Familiar object, with which one plays. There are many different balls; but the most common is stuffed with hair, *pelo*, from which it gets its name. It is round in shape and divided into quarters. One plays with it in the *trinque*, a kind of court, and that is why the small ball struck with a stringed racket is called a *trigonal*.

SEBASTIÁN DE COVARRUBIAS, 1611

The Garden
Academies

—◆—•—◆—

The popes of the Counter-Reformation were serious men,
intent on their work, with little trace of worldliness. They
put people to death in volume, preferably slowly and before an
audience, but always after a trial. They were thoroughly nepo-
tistic and they trafficked in influence as readily as one wipes
one's nose on a cold day, but they had good reason: only family
could be trusted, because if a pope left a flank exposed, any
subordinate would slit his throat without trial. They had no
mistresses or children; they wore sackcloth under their vestments; they smelled bad. They were great builders and tirelessly
checked to see that not a single breast appeared in a single
painting in any house of worship. They believed in what they
did. They would never have been seen degrading themselves, at
a tennis or fencing match; they didn't go to the queeny parties
that blared across the Tiber.

After nineteen years of ostracism, when Cardinal Montalto
emerged in a golden carriage to occupy his rooms at the Apos-
tolic Palace with the plans of the future city of Rome under his
arm, he gave his sister Camilla Peretti the Boleyn ball.

Camilla Montalto di Peretti was an elderly widow, with the

sorts of habits that might be expected of a cardinal's closest confidante, but she had daughters who—unlike her and the recently anointed Pope Sixtus V—made a life for themselves at court and played tennis: it was what was expected of young and comely millionairesses. "It's like a ball game," said Jacinto Polo de Medina in 1630 in *The Garden Academies*, referring to the personal finances of princesses, "in which women like better to take service than to give it."

Sixtus V and his sister were of truly humble origin: they were the children of a mule driver and a washerwoman and they had been orphaned early on, the ten brothers and sisters between them dead or gone. Camilla, fourteen years younger than the pope, had grown up in tow of her brother as he became altar boy, seminarist, and priest. Her first memories were of the years when he was already scaling the ties of the cardinal's mantle, spurred on by extraordinary ambition but also by the responsibility of elder brothers toward those born after them, a force of nature in itself.

It was fear of want that made her brother beat all records for the raising of palaces and the reconstruction of roads in Rome, as if to expel the phantom of poverty from the city it fell to him to govern. It was not Camilla's fate to face such a fear. She was a simple woman, who never minded acting as a kind of lady-in-waiting to Montalto, and who, though capable of enjoying the advantages of being sister to the pope, didn't lose her head over them either. If she happily assumed the duties of Vatican princess, sharing in the ostentation of the Palazzo Montalto, it is also true that once her brother crossed the Tiber and changed his name to Sixtus, she wrote to her friend Costanza Colonna to ask for a place in her loggia, more modest and easier to over-see than the monstrous mansion where Montalto had put his theories on the redesign of Rome into practice. In addition to being discreet, Camilla was a cultured woman, so she loved the idea of retiring to the medieval mansion in whose gardens the poetess Vittoria Colonna had hosted gatherings frequented by Michelangelo.

Camilla accepted the slightly battered tennis ball given to her by His Holiness and moved to the loggia with her daughters. It's funny—said her brother on one of the few occasions when he visited her after he was anointed—it was here that Pius gave me the ball that I gave you. What ball? The one made of the hair of the mad queen—do you still have it? It's here some-where. Don't lose it; it was the good-luck charm that kept me alive through the years of darkness.

Camilla had left the ball—which in truth she found a little repellent—in the rooms of the loggia's overseer: a priest of a certain rank at St. Peter's who answered to the name Pandolfo Pucci and who had been Michelangelo Merisi da Caravaggio's first employer in Rome. He'd given him work painting saints in landscapes that he later sold to village churches. None survive.

The Really
Lousy Meeting
of Two Worlds

—◆•◆—

As I've noted, Hernán Cortés was always in over his head, not least in the life he was fated to lead. He was swamped, too, by a cloak, among other juicier presents that he was given by Moctezuma's emissaries on the spot that a few days later he baptized as La Villa Rica de la Vera Cruz and that today is the town of Antigua at the mouth of the Huitzilapan River.

A few years ago, on the occasion of the five-hundredth anniversary of the discovery of America, the Spanish government commissioned a replica of the *Santa María*, Columbus's caravel from which one of the Pinzón brothers first spied Hispaniola. I saw it in Veracruz, as it happens, and later I was able to visit it in the port of Baltimore, where it was on loan for years, for reasons unknown: it was at a tourist wharf between a World War II submarine and a sumptuous, triple-masted British galleon.

The caravel was a dinghy, a limping little ship that can scarcely be believed to have held a crew of explorers on a diet of infested water, rotten beer, and damp hardtack. It was a rowboat, a nut, a little plucked bird. The brigantines with which Cortés sailed the Mexican coast from Yucatán to Veracruz before deciding to annex Mexico to the Spanish empire were even smaller. Agonizing little ships, in the holds of which the horses could barely stand upright; ships that could sail down a river, and that when tied to a tree stayed put.

The captain and his original conquistadors still looked rumpled and bleary-eyed when the emissaries of Moctezuma arrived, after following the Spaniards' ships by land from Tabasco. Cortés was absolutely not ready for a diplomatic conversation that first morning in Mexico. They've brought gold, said the soldier, whose name was Álvaro de Campos; lots of gold. Then I'm coming, said Cortés; wake Aguilar. When the captain got out of bed, setting his feet on the cabin's plank floor, there rose behind him—her hair in tangles and her skin a little bruised from the weight of his body—the face of the girl Malinalli Tenépatl, princess of Painala and courtesan of the cacique of Potonchán, skilled in arts no less valuable for being dirty. Time to use your tongue, Cortés ordered. She, whose polyglot brain was beginning to recognize simple orders in Spanish, asked in Chontal: On you or the gentleman? But seeing that Cortés was getting dressed and Álvaro de Campos wasn't getting undressed, she understood that it was her services as a translator that were required.

Cortés put on his full suit of armor and ordered that, in addition to Aguilar and Malinalli, his mouthpieces, he be joined by the fifteen horsemen distributed among the eleven brigantines that made up the expedition. The others should stay on board until further notice. He ordered that the horsemen dress as if they were riding to conquer Cempoala, with breastplates, chausses, and plumed helmets, even though this was the dry depths of spring and it was hellishly hot. From the drawer in his cabin he took one of the pearl necklaces that he had brought from Cuba in the event of an exchange of gifts, weighing it in his fist, and also took a little bracelet of green glass beads from which hung a tiny, cheap copper crucifix. He put both objects in his pocket and went down to the cargo hold to untie his horse himself.

They had to wade ashore in water up to their balls, each leading his horse with one hand and holding the ship's mooring line with the other. If the ropes had been rotten, if Cortés's glove had been new, or if he had been distracted—slapping at a mosquito on his ear—the captain might have been swept away by the current, his body ending up in the Gulf of Mexico and Spain itself falling back to Santiago de Cuba. But that didn't happen. The explorers came out sopping and bloated from the water absorbed by cloth and leather, and greeted Moctezuma's emissaries with the obeisance that they had learned very badly during their childhoods as petty wasteland nobility. One of the lieutenants, called Ricardo de los Reyes—after a town in Extremadura and not because he had the slightest trace of noble blood in him—even sat on a rock to pour the water out of his boots, for which he was castigated with a growl that, if it had survived in the dictionaries, would today be considered a Cortesian adjective.

The captain mounted his horse, as his men did theirs, and they all proceeded to the meeting hosted by the local cacique, who was witness to the first exchange between the emissaries of the two bloodiest monarchs in the world at that time.

They met in the plaza of a town with the unpronounceable name of Chalchicueyecan, and there Cortés got off his horse—

he alone—and gave the imperial ambassador an embrace of
sweat, leather, and steel. His men noted nervously that behind
the Aztec and two other Mexica diplomats stood a considerable
company of young men wearing nothing but loincloths and
cloaks in eye-popping colors, all carrying rather terrifying
weapons consisting of clubs studded with knives. No matter
how many horses the Spaniards had, they were only eighteen—
counting Malinalli, who was a child, and Aguilar, who was a
priest and quite overweight, and Cortés, who was an old man.

Aguilar and then Malinalli translated that they came in
peace, so long as the Aztecs converted to Christianity. The emissaries said yes of course, no problem. Then they set out their
gifts. This is what Moctezuma's men delivered, no matter which
chronicler is consulted:

1. A solid gold sun
2. A solid silver moon
3. More than one hundred gold and silver plates set
   with jade
4. Armbands, anklets, lip plugs
5. Miters and tiaras encrusted with blue gems like
   sapphires
6. All kinds of carved green stones
7. Harnesses, chain mail, doublets, shooting devices,
   shields
8. Plumes, fans, and capes made of feathers
9. Strange woven garments and bed hangings

Cortés thanked them for the gifts and gave them:

1. The bracelet of glass beads

Since there was a notable imbalance between the two mounds of intercontinental memorabilia, he asked a soldier by the name of Bernardo Suárez to toss him his helmet:

2. A helmet

When the swap was over—the Mexica ambassadors exchanging slightly disconcerted looks before proceeding, either because Cortés's gifts were rubbish or because they would have preferred a horse to sacrifice—Cortés made a small bow and turned his back on the imperial messengers. He was preparing to mount again when Aguilar informed him that the Aztecs had something else to add.

The main ambassador said: We bring you these valuable gifts so that you will give them to your emperor as a token of our friendship and respect; we hope that they please you and that you return to deliver them with all your men and all the terrible beasts you have brought with you; we hope that you never again set foot in our lands. Malinalli, who by now had her own agenda and preferred to be the wife of an absentminded old man than to go back to being the sex slave of a cacique and all his friends, translated this as: We bring you these very valuable gifts but in truth they are as nothing compared with what lies ahead; we hope you like them; we give them to you so that you won't even think about advancing farther with your terrible beasts because we know that the people are so unhappy with the emperor that they would surely join your cause and not ours. Aguilar, seeing the young warriors and their clubs bristling with knives, said: They give you a warm welcome; they say that they bring you these gifts from the emperor of this land, who is troubled because his people are unhappy; they say that it's best if you don't help him, that in order to get anywhere you'd have to beat all the boys over there, and they are terrible. Cortés said that he'd think about it, and everyone seemed satisfied with his response.

The conversation between the Aztecs and Spaniards continued in more or less the same vein throughout the first stage of the conquest of Mexico, which ended with the previously described stay of Cortés and his men in Tenochtitlan. There are few better illustrations of how a whole host of people can manage to understand absolutely nothing, act in an impulsive and idiotic way, and still drastically change the course of history.

Basket of Fruit

——◆•◆——

Caravaggio had a third patron in his meteoric years: Federico Borromeo, cousin of Saint Carlo and at that point the youngest cardinal Milan had ever had. He was elected at age twenty-three because, with the ideologue of the Counter-Reformation dead, it was unimaginable that Milan's cardinal seat could be occupied by a priest from another family.

Before Carlo Borromeo died—an ascetic and twisted spike, a terror, the fucking thought police *avant la lettre*—Federico had hoped to be a theology professor. His cousin's almost instant canonization came as he was editing the Acts of the Council of Trent, which meant that choosing him was a logical as well as doctrinal decision: he was the only person who really understood what the hell the Counter-Reformation was about, now that it had Europe gushing blood. Also, Federico Borromeo was a key pawn in the pope's chess game: he was on the side of the French in Milan, a city that Philip III had just seized back by force of arms for the Spanish empire.

It's not surprising, then, that in the autumn of 1599, Federico Borromeo was living in exile at the Palazzo Giustiniani in the

Piazza di San Luigi dei Francesi: he was present at the consecration of the Contarelli Chapel.

Cardinal Borromeo the Second wasn't a sanctimonious or
virtuous type—unlike the banker whose guest he was, he was a
regular at his neighbor's men-only masked balls—but he had a
sainted last name to preserve.

Borromeo had his own collection of art, tasteful and well
chosen, which was deposited in the Ambrosian Library upon
his death. Unlike his cousin the saint, who left a trail of misery
across Europe, Federico spent his time and money buying books
and manuscripts his agents sent him from Greece and Syria for
the library on antiquity he founded, which exists to this day. It's
to him that we owe much of our knowledge of the Hellenes.

When Borromeo the Second arrived in Rome, in small part
to represent the interests of Milan at the Vatican and in large
part because he definitely was not welcome by the Spanish government in his native city, Caravaggio had yet to turn to painting only what and as he liked: he was about to abandon the
background noise of bucolic Mannerism that still suffused his
sacred scenes before the absolute triumph of his *Calling of Saint
Matthew*. Borromeo was his first private client: he bought a
lesser painting, *Basket of Fruit*, before Caravaggio set the history
of art on fire with the reds of *Judith Beheading Holofernes*.

Basket of Fruit was painted not as fruit appears in nature, but
rather as it looks reflected from a certain distance in a concave
mirror. In its time, the painting was considered a virtuosic work
more in the manner of the Flemish artists than the Italians.
Rather than represent a window with foreshortening toward the

outside, as Renaissance optical realism tended to do, it occupied an interior three-dimensional space: to look at it was to see a basket on a shelf. To heighten the effect, Caravaggio painted the background the same color as the wall in Borromeo's study at the Palazzo Giustiniani and even followed the small cracks and bulgings in the wall on which it hung. The background must have been painted in situ.

Painting the fruit, which was on the verge of rotting, couldn't have taken Caravaggio more than two days of work in his studio. The piece measures twelve by nineteen inches, which means that it crossed the Piazza di San Luigi dangling from the artist's fingertips by the upper inside stretcher of the mounted canvas, as the main figure was already drying. Merisi must have carried his paintbrushes and palette in the other hand, his mind fixed on how to reproduce the quality of light on the texture of a real wall.

The painting, likely transported with his usual air of provocation, was a revolutionary object in a way that those of us living afterward can't imagine, because it's always been present and we've seen it reproduced a thousand times without even realizing it. Not only does the perspective extend out into the room in which it's hung, but no Italian artist had ever painted a still life before—that's why the painting is called *Basket of Fruit*: the idea of a "still life" had yet to be conceived.

The artist must have entered the Palazzo Giustiniani by the entrance to the servant's courtyard after midday—the light reflected on the wall isn't white, but orangish, like Roman light on autumn afternoons. He must have passed the stable doors and come in through the kitchen. Surely he blew away the hair falling over his face before beginning the climb up the servants' stairs. Then he must have arranged his cloak before going through the false wall that connected the lower realms with the *piano nobile*, pushing the door open with his hip. The office must have been made ready for him to do his work while Borromeo attended to business at the government offices of the Vatican.

It was there in Borromeo's study that Caravaggio saw the object that changed his sense of color: one of the miters that a strange bishop by the name of Vasco de Quiroga, radical and possibly brilliant, had brought as a gift for Pope Paul III when he was called to the Council of Trent.

Iridescence

—◆•◆—

With the first—very brief—diplomatic exchange concluded, Cortés called for chests to stow the gifts for Charles V in one of the brigantines. While they were being packed and inventoried, the captain's gaze fell on one of the mantles. He liked it because it was full of motifs: it told a story of butterflies, corn plants, snails, rivers, squash. It was a cluttered and mysterious tale constructed in shades of brown by an artist who could embroider with great delicacy and skill. That can't be worth much, he said to the soldier who was acting as notary; take it to my house when you're done. You don't have a house, the soldier replied. Well, build me one, here, and he pointed to a spot on the ground. The men, including Jerónimo de Aguilar, turned to look at him. And disembark the rest of the troops; tonight we'll sleep on land.

By nighttime, the brown mantle that the captain had decided to keep was padding his hammock, which was slung between two of four posts covered by a roof of palm leaves: the first outpost of a European captain in continental America. If Julius Caesar traveled with his library, why shouldn't I camp with my coverlet, thought Cortés, as he gazed disinterestedly at Malinalli. She was trying to explain to him in gestures that this wasn't a cloak or a coverlet but a mantle, much more valuable than most of the objects that had been inventoried, and that if Moctezuma had decided to heap gifts on his king, this was the very thing he should send: the rest was filler.

He fucked her under Moctezuma's royal mantle. Then he pulled it over himself and slept splendidly. It took Malinalli a few more hours to fall asleep, overwhelmed as she was by the value of the imperial object covering her. Sleep came only when she realized that sleeping under a king's mantle had been her original destiny.

Hernán Cortés's second day in Mexico was slow and—due to the order he'd given his men always to go about in full armor—sticky. He spent it pacing the borders of what in his mind was already a Spanish, or at least a Cuban, town—and what in the minds of his men was a pit of snakes and giant insects that had to be cleared of brush for no evident reason. The captain was cross, so no one could work up the courage to ask why he had decided to set up camp rather than continue exploring the coast.

When the main street of what would become the town of La Villa Rica de la Vera Cruz was clear and the posts of the soldiers' barracks were raised, the captain ordered that a church be built next to the shelter in which he had slept the night before. The altar wall must be of adobe, he said; so that Aguilar can say mass with dignity. He silenced the stirrings of mutiny by ordering that they also unload the barrels of beer they'd brought from Cuba. Today we'll eat like kings, he said.

He had reviewed his provisions and seen that they had enough to survive for ten or twelve days. And yet this land was so rich that they could spend as if they'd come into a fortune. To add to the spread, Malinalli found sweet-water shrimp in Chalchicueyecan, in addition to two Indian women who would make tortillas for the troops and corn masa for the chocolate drink called *pozol*.

When Cortés asked her that night what she'd done to make the Indians so generous, she let slip via Aguilar the idea that changed the world: I told them that we were here to overthrow their tyrant, that with our horses and their arrows we could liberate them from the yoke of the Aztecs.

On his third day in Mexico, Cortés didn't even visit the site where the church was being built: he spent it talking to residents of the nearby village in the company of his mouthpieces. He walked all over the town, visited its fields, and took refreshment with its cacique, who offered men to help finish the church sooner. Cortés and Aguilar agreed that this offer of workmen was clear proof of the first Veracruzans' readiness to embrace the true faith, even though the cacique, after lending them his people's labor, begged them to please tie up their fearsome dogs and horses in exchange.

Toward evening, Cortés found the members of the expedition gloomier than in previous days. They had made better progress thanks to the arrival of the Indians, but the unhealthiness of the region was killing them: two soldiers were already down with fever, and a dog had been devoured alive by the insects. How to go on like this, Captain, asked the soldier Álvaro de Campos.

He let them have beer again and holed up in his shelter to do things with Malinalli. That night she told him in signs that she wanted to remove the mantle from the hammock and hang it from the posts of La Capitana—that was the name of their hut now. It wasn't that she thought their quarters would be improved by decoration, but at least her new owner would stop staining such a precious object with semen and slobber. He shrugged and said she could do what she liked, pulling the mantle over himself. She understood that she'd won the latest argument in what was beginning to seem more and more like a marriage than an arrangement between owner and slave.

The next morning Malinalli hung the piece as soon as Cortés had gone off to work raising the chapel with his men and the Indians. His presence on the site surely dampened complaints, but it didn't fully stop the bellyaching: a Spaniard in disagreement is a Spaniard who grumbles no matter the circumstances. That night, once the camp was raised and the beer was flowing, Cortés said to a soldier by the name of Alberto Caro: Do you think there'll be a rebellion if I ask them to build the gate to the chapel out of stone? The beer won't last forever, Caro replied. The captain insisted: Poor Aguilar hasn't said mass in a real church since he was taken by the Chontal; don't you think it's a good cause? As far as I'm concerned, Aguilar can go back to the jungle, said Caro. But it would keep them busy, Cortés protested. Busy, said the soldier; what for? What we should do, he continued in a tone that could have been considered mutinous in a serious military encampment, is get back on board ship and keep exploring. The captain shrugged his shoulders in response and said: Tomorrow I'll decide.

That night, Malinalli was in a splendid mood when Cortés got back to La Capitana. With everyone away building the chapel, Aguilar had seized the chance to baptize her in the brush and bestow upon her the Christian name of Marina. He had given her a certificate of baptism, plainly improvised but no less valid for that, which she in turn gave to her master. Doña Marina? What is that supposed to mean, said Cortés when he read it. He sent for the priest.

Aguilar explained that the girl had been a princess before she became the servant of his passions and that royal blood was royal blood; now that she was baptized she couldn't be his slave, though if they wanted to they could agree to live together under common law. What does that mean, asked Don Hernando. That you can take her back to Cuba and let your wife go fuck herself; it's all legal. Would you come with us? Not on your life, it'll be back to Yucatán for me. Will you say a mass of thanksgiving in that dump of a chapel those incompetents are building for you? Thanksgiving for what? Please. I'll do whatever you tell me to do.

Back at La Capitana, Marina waited for the explorer, prepared to give him the only gift she could as someone newly freed, with nothing else in the world but her body. She stood completely naked, lit by the glow of a beeswax candle with a wick made of her own hair. This voluntary surrender greatly excited the conquistador, who immediately fell on his knees to bury his nose between her thighs. She sat in the hammock, spread her legs, and thrust her pelvis forward to feel his facial hair on her sex: the attentions of a man with a beard still drove her wild. She put her hand in his matted hair. Cortés loved the taste of Malinalli because she was young, she bathed every morning, and she ate flowers. She lay back in the hammock, holding it still to coddle her orgasm: her legs parted, her arms flung wide, her tits pointing up to the palm ceiling. To come, she hooked her shins over the captain's shoulders, doubling over him. Then she lay back again in the hammock. It was only now that Cortés, on his knees, looked up and saw the commotion stirred in Moctezuma's mantle, lit by the candle stub.

The finely worked stuff that he had so admired, and that had made him decide to keep the mantle, was glowing. The birds soared, shining as if with a light of their own, the rays leading back to the sun traced on the mantle; the butterflies were each of a different color; the ears of corn seemed to rustle in the breeze at the twinkling of the candle stub; what had looked like squash were the faces of men and women, mixed in their perfect earthiness with plants, snails, and animals that he had never even noticed before. Fish undulated underwater. It was raining. I told you so, Malinalli whispered in his ear in Chontal. She bit his mouth.

The next morning the captain made an appearance at the breakfast of the troops, which now definitively included the Indians who had arrived only to work as carpenters. As he rolled a tortilla with a mash of ants, flowers, and chili, he said casually: We have to finish the walls of the chapel today so that Aguilar can consecrate it; then we'll send the gifts for the emperor off to Cuba and we'll begin to dismantle the other ten brigantines. The men forgot their food—ants escaping from the tacos—to stare at him with goggle eyes. We'll need the wood and the metal. Álvaro de Campos was the only one brave enough to ask: Why?

We're off to conquer Tenochtitlan, fool.

Third Set, First Game

—◆•◆—

The Lombard looked at the poet from where they both lay sprawled on the ground. He raised his eyebrows in greeting. The Spaniard responded in kind. It was the first time since the night before that they'd had an exchange that wasn't at the end of a racket.

The artist sat up and wiped the blood from his face, rolling his head from side to side, and finally stood. Immediately he advanced toward his opponent and offered him his hand. The poet took it without hesitation and the scapular fell from his shirt as he got up. The Lombard took it in his hand and tilted it back and forth. I've seen something like this before, he said; what is it? A scapular. No, the image, what is the image made of? I don't know, said the Spaniard; it comes from the New World. The artist looked at it for a moment longer and then let it go: Have you seen how it reflects the light? The poet didn't understand the question. He tucked it back into his shirt.

The Lombard put his arm over the Spaniard's shoulder and whispered in his ear: Do you remember why we're playing; the professor told me it's a duel, but he didn't say why. The poet nodded. If he could have, he would have prolonged the feeling of his rival's breath on his ear. He exhaled visibly, shaking off the artist on the pretext of rubbing his left shoulder, which hurt after the scramble of the race. He said: Wipe your face, it's still bleeding. The Italian rubbed his cheek with his sleeve: black as it was and worn for who knows how many days, it showed nothing. If only we could take a break and have something to drink, he said; some wine with water. The Spaniard smiled. It would only make things worse. Seeing the movements of his opponent from up close, his face that of an ordinary man, not an animal adversary, his heart almost softened. Let's finish this thing and be done with it, he said. The artist shrugged and crossed the court before the duke and the professor stretched the cord.

The night before, the Spaniards had come late from a brothel to the Tavern of the Bear, where they were staying. They were in excellent humor, their manhoods and bellies satisfied. Before retiring to their rooms, they had stopped in on the lower floor, by now in the silly state of those who have already had too much to drink.

The place was empty except for a gang of wastrels, who were drinking and taking up much more space than they needed and making much more noise than was normal even for a Roman drunken outing. The group consisted of six or seven layabouts, a young man with the air of a priest and an old man's beard, and what looked like a soldier: a wiry man, dressed in black, with a pointed mustache and a beard in the French style. He was the only one wearing dagger and sword.

The Spaniards kept to themselves: they knew that half of Rome was on the side of France and had had enough of King Philip. Also, they were in the city fleeing from justice and had drunk and fucked enough that they had no more energy left to burn. They were relaxed. The Italians, on the other hand, gesticulated and roared with laughter.

It was Otero who had established contact with them, without quite meaning to. He had gotten up for a second flask of wine, and at the bar he had noticed the slightly hunched young man with the distinguished beard—plainly trustworthy—ordering a flask of grappa for his table. Otero asked in his meager Italian what it was, and the other man responded in easy Spanish that it was *orujo*. He asked the innkeeper for a cup and filled it, handing it to Otero with a smile. Try it, he said. Otero, who had drunk God knows how much *orujo* in his soldier's life, took a sip and felt an enormous pleasure: when grappa is good, there is a near-irresistible burst of light in the hypothalamus. He asked to exchange his wine for a flask of the silky *orujo* he had tried, and brought it back to the table, saying a polite goodbye to the man who had treated him to a glass before he returned to his seat. They drank it quickly.

The Spaniards were exchanging some final nonsense before going up to bed on the floor above when the innkeeper arrived with two more jugs of grappa. One is on the house and the other is on the gentlemen over there, he said, setting them down so hard they sloshed. The duke and the poet looked at each other without saying anything: two bottles of grappa was a serious undertaking in the state they were in. Osuna thanked the innkeeper, filled his men's cups, and raising the jug in the direction of the Italians he toasted them, and took a long swig. The gesture—one group of cavemen to another—was heartily cheered by the locals, who soon invited them to pull up a chair.

The poet was already bouncing the ball, eager more than anything for the match to be over, when the duke cried with an authority that he hadn't displayed until this point in the match: Where are you going so fast? The poet turned to look at him, raising his eyebrows. His linesman beckoned him over to the gallery. The Italians didn't miss their chance: they whistled. The artist scratched his head theatrically with his racket and his second rolled his eyes up toward the roof beams.

What the hell do you plan to do, asked the duke. Hold out, the poet replied; use the wall, wear him down. Fine, said the duke, and then added, jerking his right thumb at Otero's men: They're asking what you were talking about to that faggot at the changeover. The escorts snorted uncomfortably. I don't remember asking a thing, said Barral. Well, then I'm asking, what did you talk about? We talked about the scapular, the heat, nothing. You have to beat him, you can't give up; what I say goes here, and I say you have to win.

The poet rested his forehead on the railing. He shook his head a few times and then returned to the baseline. He shouted *Tenez!* and hit a miserable shot, which scarcely struck the roof before floating down to the other side of the court. The artist didn't go after it. He watched it with a weary look, with impatience, with all the infinite scorn that a creature at once so savage and sophisticated could muster for a kid of nineteen, a Spaniard in the service of a ridiculous grandee, and shouted: Send me something real. Fifteen–love, shouted the duke, furious because he too had noticed the poet's erection from the friction of the race: Love, one way or another.

He served again, more decisively, and the artist, before driving the ball back, asked in a repugnant voice: *Fatto tutto, spagnolo?* He swiveled his hips, moving with feminine cruelty. It wasn't a great send-up, but it got a roar from the crowd—even the Spanish guards laughed. The poet took it short and put it in a corner. Thirty–love, shouted the duke. And addressing Otero: Would you laugh at your own mother, cocksucker? The mercenaries exchanged glances.

The third serve was diabolical. The artist reached it far from the baseline and hit a short return, setting the poet up for a slice. The Italian still managed to return it, but on the next stroke the ball dropped at the other end of the court and he didn't have the will to chase it. When the duke cried *Juego para Castilla,* the poet's face was full of thunder.

Love That Doesn't Speak Its Name

————•————

There is a painting from the early seventeenth century called *The Death of Hyacinth*. Though attributed for a time to Merisi, today it is believed to be the work of one of his disciples, probably Cecco del Caravaggio. In it, Hyacinth and Apollo are depicted at the moment of the former's death. If Saint Sebastian in all his arrow-pierced ecstasy hadn't become the patron saint of gay culture, it's likely that Hyacinth would today be the emblematic mythological figure of male homosexuality.

Friend and lover of Apollo, Hyacinth was the son of Clio and a Macedonian or Peloponnesian king—depending on who tells the tale, he was either Macedonian or Spartan. The god, deeply in love with the hero, was training him in the stadium arts when he tossed him the discus with divine strength and inadvertently killed him. He wept so much and so vigorously that his tears transformed Hyacinth's body into the flower that bears his name, which prevented Hades from carrying him away to the underworld.

In classical representations of the myth, which in ancient Greece was associated with the passage from adolescence to adulthood, Zephyr, god of the wind, rises up with Hyacinth to save him from hell. The specialist term for the posture in which they rise is *intercrural coitus*—that is, a kind of coitus in which there is no penetration, and orgasm is produced by the friction of the genitalia on the thighs of the two participants.

Cecco del Caravaggio was the most loyal of the Caravaggisti, painters who imitated Merisi until the star of his art faded. And he was the only one of them who worked in Merisi's studio and accompanied him on most of the escapades that made him infamous as a man with a tendency for insubordination, for conduct that defied the norm of the city of the popes, and—inevitably—for crime. Cecco's nudes depicting Love laughing raucously or Saint John the Baptist as a young man are still provocative in their frontal frankness.

In the painting of the death of Hyacinth—a subject later also taken up by Tiepolo—Apollo weeps for his lover. Instead of the discus of the original myth, he is carrying a racket in his hand. At the feet of the hero, a hyacinth blooms next to his own tennis racket—a fallen bird.

Ex
———•———

Hernán Cortés returned from the expedition to Las Hibueras a year and a half after giving the order to garrote Cuauhtémoc, and after bestowing a Spanish husband and the town of Orizaba on Marina. Of the three thousand five hundred men with whom he claimed what would later be called Honduras, he returned with only eighty, all of them Spanish. The Indians—always the overwhelming majority in his armies—had fulfilled what may have been their sacred destiny, hearing the bark of three thousand four hundred and twenty dogs in the night and following through sickness and war their last emperor to his death. Surely many of them, upon finding themselves in strange lands that couldn't even be conquered because there were no empires to fight, simply took to the bush and swore off the ridiculousness of being Christians and vassals of Charles V.

The expedition to Las Hibueras had been a grand failure. There was the precipitous stretch of Guatemalan mountain on which, between those that were lamed or fled into the wild and those that plunged over the edge, sixty-eight horses were lost. There was hunger. There were ambushes. During one of them, an arrow struck Cortés in the head; no convincing explanation exists of how it was removed and how he was able to carry on. There were illnesses and no Tlaxcalan shaman girls to cure them, only cantankerous old Mayan women to make them worse.

The lives of Cortés and eighty of his thousands of men were saved because at some point on the Honduran coast they found a well-provisioned Spanish ship. The conquistador bought it on credit—lock, stock, and barrel, including the crew—and continued the expedition by sea. Upon his return he even allowed himself the privilege of stopping by Cuba to see his friends, returning to Veracruz plumper and in clean clothes.

He spent the first night of the trip back to Mexico City in Orizaba. There, La Malinche paid a polite visit to the conquistador at the house of the town elder, where he was staying. They sat at the table and talked: bitter enemies now, like all those who have slept together long and well but no longer share a bed. He lied about the success of his expedition and the importance of the three port cities he had founded and let die. She said—as all ex-wives say—that she was glad to be out from under the thumb of a man past his prime, that it was their son—named Martín, of course—whom she missed, though he hadn't been to visit her despite all the messages and gifts she had sent him. Finally, she handed him the sparrow woven from the hair of the last Aztec emperor. What is it, asked Cortés. After his bouts of fever in the jungles of El Petén, he sometimes forgot things. The scapular you asked me for, said Marina. Cortés smelled it, then held it out before him. You haven't worn it, he said. I'd have to be crazy. On the face of the pendant was not the silver medallion that the conquistador had sent to her on the day Cuauhtémoc died, but an image in featherwork of the Virgin of Guadalupe. Cortés kissed the image, tilted it until he found the point at which it glowed with refracted light, and smiled with a sincerity that he could come by only very infrequently now. Thank you, he said, clutching it in his fist. He put it on.

When the bard Lope Rodríguez found him lying dead in his house in Castilleja de la Cuesta, outside Seville, he removed it from around his neck. He had never taken it off.

Theft

⸺ • ⸺

In 1620, the doctor and artists' biographer Giulio Mancini devoted an entry in his book *Considerazioni sulla pittura* to Michelangelo Merisi da Caravaggio, whom he had once treated after a rather flamboyant accident involving knife slashes and horse kicks. The brief biography of the artist begins like this: "Our age owes much to the art of Merisi."

From Giulio Mancini we learn that Caravaggio had reached Rome in 1592, at the age of twenty-one. He went to live at the loggia of the Colonna family and was employed by Camilla Montalto, sister of Pope Sixtus V. The artist must have come to her on the recommendation of Princess Costanza Colonna, who had employed his father as a master stonemason in Milan. The Lombardy noblewoman had always shown a great weakness for Caravaggio: she had protected him as a boy during the terrible plague that took his father, and spent her life applying for work and clemency for him at his frequent request.

It's no surprise, either, that the Colonnas were interested in introducing a painter into the explosive city of Rome at the end of the sixteenth century. Lombardy had turned out great bankers, brilliant generals, and pedigreed priests, but its status wouldn't be secure for all eternity if it didn't also furnish a native of Milan capable of decorating the walls of a Roman church.

Caravaggio was a painter of undistinguished images of saints during the period in which he lived in the Colonna loggia. Camilla Montalto put him to work for Pandolfo Pucci, the miserable bastard priest who made him paint in return for sustenance that scarcely deserved the name: in his household, the servants ate nothing but lettuce.

Says Mancini: "Salad for the first course, the main dish, dessert, and even for toothpicks." On Caravaggio's already formidable drunken sprees, compensation for the rigors of trying to make a life as a young artist in a city to which all the young artists of Europe had already moved, he would call his patron "Monsignor Insalata." The fact that Mancini knew this suggests that in his own youth he must have been something less than a paragon of good behavior.

Naturally, Merisi soon left the service of Camilla Montalto and her Monsignor Insalata. Before he left, he took the Boleyn ball as recompense. He wasn't interested only in its chest, which he surely sold off cheap to a cut-rate jeweler. Next to painting, *pallacorda* was the great passion of his life and a source of income.

It was his dirty-nailed fingers that emerged from the field of ashes left by the blaze of the Counter-Reformation, only instead of opening to the sun like a butterfly of flesh, they snatched up the ball, hiding it away in a pocket.

Priests Who
Were Swine

❖━━•━━❖

Vasco de Quiroga, the first bishop of Michoacán, received his invitation to the renewed sessions of the Council of Trent in cassock sleeves. If in 1521 the nose of Hernán Cortés's horse marked the farthest reach of the Holy Roman Empire, by 1538 the Aztecs were already as lost and mythical a people as the Atlanteans or the Garamantes, and their genetic material lay at the bottom of Lake Texcoco, or had been circulated for the last time through the lungs of those who breathed in the smoke of the huge piles of bodies burned after the fall of Tenochtitlan. We Mexicans aren't descendants of the Mexicas, but of the nations that joined with Cortés to overthrow them. We're a country whose name is the product of nostalgia and guilt.

In 1537—the year Bishop Quiroga received an invitation, signed and sealed by Pope Paul III, to the Council of Trent— the Purépecha, historic and never-defeated enemies of the Aztecs, had themselves been decapitated by the Spanish conquistadors. The war was extraordinarily neat, because there was only one contender: the conquistadors. The Purépecha, knowing that there was no way to withstand the attack of all the nations of Mesoamerica, who were unified for the first time under the cannon-fire command of the Europeans, had yielded without firing a single arrow at their new masters, and their emperor had been baptized. In exchange for this surrender, all they asked was to maintain the kingdom's integrity. Their request was granted—the kingdom of Nueva Galicia, which stretched from the Balsas River to Sinaloa, was nominally independent from New Spain during the sixteenth century—but the emperor and the entirety of the governing and military classes were exterminated in dishonorable and savage fashion by the armies of the traitor Nuño Beltrán de Guzmán, second governor of New Spain and a conquistador of Michoacán. By 1538, the year Vasco de Quiroga received the invitation to Trent, Guzmán was already in jail, serving a sentence—hopefully painful—for murder, theft, and cowardice.

In those days, the leading edge of the Holy Roman Empire was no longer a weapon or a horse but rather the spine of Vasco de Quiroga's copy of *Utopia*; Europe extended as far as he could point with his book. Let's put a metalworks here, the bishop said to the Indians—who loved him so much they called him Tata, "Grandfather"—and pointed to a field with the spine of his tome. What sprang up—though the Indians didn't realize it, and Vasco de Quiroga may not have, either—was a new branch of the sheltering tree that the Holy Roman Empire also aspired to be, and sometimes was. Build me a school here; a hospital. The spine of *Utopia*. Another branch.

As I write, I don't know what this book is about. It's not exactly about a tennis match. Nor is it a book about the slow and mysterious integration of America into what we call "the Western world"—an outrageous misapprehension, since from the

American perspective, Europe is the East. Maybe it's just a book about how to write this book; maybe that's what all books are about. A book with a lot of back-and-forth, like a game of tennis.

It isn't a book about Caravaggio or Quevedo, though Caravaggio and Quevedo are in the book, as are Cortés and Cuauhtémoc, and Galileo and Pius IV. Gigantic individuals facing off. All fucking, getting drunk, gambling in the void. Novels demolish monuments because all novels, even the most chaste, are a tiny bit pornographic.

Nor is it a book about the birth of tennis as a popular sport, though it definitely has its roots in extensive research that I conducted on the subject with a grant at the New York Public Library. I embarked on the research after mulling over the discovery of a fascinating bit of information: The first truly modern painter in history was also a great tennis player and a murderer. Our brother.

Nor is it a book about the Counter-Reformation, but it takes place in a time that now goes by that name, which is why it's a book that features twisted and bloodthirsty priests, sex-addict priests who fucked children for sport, thieving priests who obscenely swelled their coffers with the tithing and alms of the poor all over the world. Priests who were swine.

Vasco de Quiroga was a good priest. A man of the world who became a man of God when his circumstances demanded it; not exactly the God in whose name everyone stole and murdered in Rome, Spain, and America, but a better one, who unfortunately doesn't exist either.

Carlo Borromeo annihilated the Renaissance by turning torture into the only way to practice Christianity. He was declared a saint the instant he died. Vasco de Quiroga saved a whole world single-handedly and died in 1565, and the process of his canonization has yet to begin. I don't know what this book is about. I know that as I wrote it I was angry because the bad guys always win. Maybe all books are written simply because in every game the bad guys have the advantage and that is too much to bear.

Third Set,
Second Game

The Spaniards gathered their winnings for the second time,
and the Romans whistled for the artist to return to the
match. Crush him and get it over with, said Saint Matthew;
we're thirsty.

Upon the merging of the two tables at the Tavern of the Bear
the night before, the poet had tried to make conversation with
the man with the venerable beard, who seemed clearly to be of
his own social class. The poet had no success, in part because
this conversation partner was clearly the timid sort, and in part
because the dominance of the *capotavola* over the group was absolute and permitted no diversions: he decided who would be
mocked and he decreed who would get the drinks. He wasn't a
petty tyrant, just the man who was paying. Under other circumstances, none of the recent arrivals would have been comfortable
with this system, but by now the alcohol had done its work and
it had been a while since they had crossed the threshold beyond
which everything seems bearable so long as the possibility remains of downing another drink.

The poet shouted *Tenez!* He tossed the ball into the air and
put all his newly recovered self-esteem into the serve. The artist

returned to the game lacking the lethal focus of the previous set, but with enough energy to maintain a tight back-and-forth on the court, obliging the Spaniard to run time and again after the ball. The perfection of the exchange was broken by the Lombard, who at some point felt that he had a better read of the shifting forces on the court and risked a merciless drive aimed at the dedans. He missed, leaving the Spaniard to wait for the rebound. The Italian had all the time in the world to rush back, bide his time, and knock the ball just inside the cord. *Amore–quindici*, cried the mathematician, even before the Spaniard wore himself out trying to reach it.

Not only did the young man dressed as a professor—for reasons unknown at that late hour and in a tavern—not talk, but the poet soon noticed that he didn't touch his cup, full to the brim since they'd all sat down at the table. Though he had an absent and taciturn look about him, every once in a while he would exchange glances with the *capotavola* that seemed to pass judgment on something just said. At this point the poet had opted to tackle the more complicated task of making conversation with the *capo* himself. It wasn't easy, since he was already engaged in preaching vulgarities to his acolytes.

After the Spaniard's second serve, the Lombard stopped trying to make the game fun. The poet lost heart when the artist brilliantly blocked a return, smiling from ear to ear, raising his racket with disdain, and letting the ball simply bounce off it and drop. The poet didn't even try to go after it, chastened by the cackles with which the beggars and tarts had crowned his effort at the end of the last point. The artist grabbed his testicles with his left hand and blew the poet a kiss.

The night before, after three boring cups of grappa, and the professor and the *capotavola* both resisting conversation, the poet had made as if to rise. Then he'd felt a steely hand on his thigh: the captain of the drunkards smiled at him with genuine innocence, blew his hair out of his eyes, and said in Italian: Excuse me, but someone has to control these savages or they'll end up wrecking the place. The poet offered his hand and the artist took it between his, giving it a manly squeeze. They're my friends, he said; awful, every one of them, but you won't find better; what are you doing in Rome? Not much, the poet answered in his rather academic Italian; visiting the holy places, letting things cool off at home. Ah, the *capo* replied with a sinister and irresistible gleam in his eye; you're fleeing because you've committed some atrocity against King Philip. More or less.

In the gallery there was a volcanic rumble: upset by the artist's crotch-grabbing and kiss, the duke's mercenaries all drew their swords and would have stormed the court and put an end to the painter's career forever if their master hadn't halted them with a sign. The Italians in the stands pulled their daggers from their breeches and crowded behind the mathematician, who spread his arms to hold them back without taking his eyes off the duke. The Spaniards didn't resume their charge, but nor did they sheathe their swords. The poet dropped his racket, and the artist had time to wonder whether he was simply stunned by the sudden outbreak of violence or whether he wanted his right hand free to run to the gallery for his sword. He calculated that he could defend himself with his racket until he reached his own weapon, which the professor didn't dare pick up from the ground but was nudging with the toe of his boot. For an instant, not a bird flew over Rome.

Under other circumstances the poet would have explained to the *capotavola* that being fugitives from justice didn't necessarily make them allies of the king of France, but with his tongue thickened by grappa, he could never have articulated it in Italian, nor was he capable by that point of rational thought. And there was something fascinating about the man who filled his cup again without letting go of his leg, in a gesture that spoke more of generosity than courtesy, because he was as rough as a brick.

The duke cried: Love–thirty, and returned to his seat. The poet took this to mean that he should keep playing, and he picked up his racket from the ground, going to retrieve the ball amid the deadly silence of the men in the gallery, who were watching him with hilts in their hands. He headed to the baseline.

Tenez! he shouted, but he waited to toss the ball into the air, giving the artist time to return to his position. He served. They knocked the ball back and forth until blades were returned to sheaths and the spectators were in their seats again. The poet felt as if his side had won this hand and they had the moral advantage after the way the duke had quieted his men. When he saw that everyone was absorbed in the match again, he attacked a high ball with abandon and drove it into the very corner of the baseline. Even the artist acknowledged with a nod that it had been a perfect stroke. *Quindici–trenta,* cried the professor in a display of courtesy to match the duke's peacemaking spirit.

Past a certain point, the occurrences of the previous night were not entirely clear in the poet's mind, though he was still too young to forget them entirely—alcohol-induced amnesia is a blessing decanted gradually with age. He had probably been embroiled in some foolish conversation with the *capo* that both found utterly gripping. He hadn't the faintest idea what they had talked about, but they had laughed, each gripping the other's shoulder every so often to explain something crucial, forehead to forehead, weeping tears of mirth.

The game is yours, the duke said when the poet went to retrieve the ball to serve again. He was taking his place behind the line, spinning the ball in his hand, when he saw his linesman order Barral to go up and place a bet, to bring things entirely back to normal. He lowered his racket, wiped his forehead. New bets. *Tenez!* The artist put up a serious fight, but he lost the point. Tie, shouted the duke.

The Spaniard was a clever and rapid-fire talker when sober; drunk, his biting commentary took on a brilliant histrionic spin: he imitated voices, pulled faces, could draw out barbs of unimaginable cruelty in a joke. The *capo* wasn't as loquacious, he was almost serious, but his way of railing against anything he didn't like, which was almost everything, was unexpectedly charming. He threw his hands up, flung back his head, and flicked the hair from his face with the arrogance of a master of Rome. There was something hypnotic about his voice, though it issued from lips too sharply drawn.

The betting went up. The poet served forcefully, then returned the artist's volley so hard that the strings of his racket almost broke. The ball was unreachable where it bounced. *Punto di cacce*, cried the professor.

He remembered laughing so hard it hurt, arms around the shoulders of his new best friend, as Italians and Spaniards tried to sing songs in unison that should definitely have been sung on their own. He remembered himself listening as intently as a child to stories that the Lombard whispered in his ear: his hot breath, the tickle of his patchy beard on his cheeks. There was always plenty of grappa.

Then he had felt the urge to piss, and stood up. Having lost the ability to get words out, he clapped the *capo* on the back to indicate that he would return. The *capo* turned to look at him. Come back soon, he said. The poet bent down and kissed him on the crown of the head. A brotherly kiss between drunks who've been having a wonderful time together. The smell of the Lombard's mass of oily hair transported him to a world in which it was perfectly possible to live without fear of persecution by King Philip's bailiffs; a world of men who risked everything and waited for death with teeth bared; a whole world in which each thing had a corresponding other.

Though the artist seemed wholly focused on chasing the ball, the poet never failed to respond with solvency and clarity. A slip by the Lombard on a low stroke brought victory to the poet. Game to Spain, cried the duke, with vehemence.

Wait, said the *capo*; I have to piss too.

Counter-Reformation

◆ • ◆

B y 1530, when Vasco de Quiroga arrived in New Spain, Tenochtitlan had been pacified. It was a city whose official language was still Nahuatl and where no one stopped to wonder anymore whether this thing with the Spaniards would be a temporary occupation or they were here to stay: yet another tribe that would govern until expelled by the next one.

The rest of infinite America still had no inkling that over the next two hundred years, dozens of thousand-year-old cultures that had flourished in isolation, without contamination or means of defense, would inexorably be trashed. Not that it matters: nothing matters. Species are extinguished, children leave home, friends turn up with impossible girlfriends, cultures disappear, languages are one day no longer spoken; those who survive convince themselves that they were the most fit.

In the third decade of the sixteenth century, the capital of the Tenochcas was the tip of a triangle that spread its arms toward the Gulf of Mexico and reached all the way to Spain. Outside the Holy Roman Empire's triangle of influence, the conquistadors must have been perceived by the majorities that surrounded them as a tribe with an inevitably superior technology of death, but also with less of a thirst for blood than the previous occupants of Mexico's imperial capital. Not that the recent arrivals were humanists on a mission to improve anyone's life, but at least they didn't make sacrifices to frenzied and glamorous gods—lovers of spectacle and gore like none before or since. Their sacrifices were to a bland and pragmatic god called money, statistically more lethal than the four divine Tezcatlipocas put together, but also slower in its means of causing harm.

Vasco de Quiroga was a lawyer of noble birth, schooled in what the court of Charles V considered the Orient, since he had been a judge in Algeria. Because of this experience, he was sent along with other less cosmopolitan judges—*oidores*, they were called medievally—to bring order to the cynical, thieving, disobedient, and murderous administration of New Spain.

Quiroga had no immediate interest in the Purépecha territory of Mechuacán, west of Mexico City, recently acquired by the Spanish crown. But he must have read and heard many accounts of the destruction of the only empire that had always withstood Aztec onslaughts.

In his first year in New Spain, Quiroga was simply a learned and circumspect judge with an astonishing capacity for work, a notable curiosity about the affairs of the indigenous culture languishing in the city, and little or no interest in playing politics. Disenchanted with the class of landowners who thus far had shared among them the governance of New Spain, Quiroga made friends among the clergy. He was a frequent visitor of Bishop Fray Juan de Zumárraga, who one day—probably when they'd been discussing how to govern the vast territory they didn't even understand—loaned him a little book written by an Englishman: *Utopia*.

It's funny that it was Juan de Zumárraga, ever eager to torture Indians and burn them at the stake, who planted the idea in Judge Quiroga's head that the indigenous peoples, self-governed in rational fashion, could turn the bone-crushing land that was New Spain into a productive and egalitarian paradise. It's no exaggeration to say that Zumárraga was a war criminal, a blood-thirsty beast, a crazy drug-cartel boss. The zeal with which he persecuted the native Americans for heresy was so scandalous that Charles V himself had to sign a decree indicating that In-dians couldn't be heretics because they were new converts, and prohibiting them from being put on trial by the Inquisition.

If Carlo Borromeo was the very incarnation of the ideology of the Counter-Reformation, Fray Juan de Zumárraga was his sharpest instrument on the other side of the world. Both of them were bishops consecrated—perhaps irresponsibly—by Pope Pius IV, who, as the last Renaissance sybarite, slayed one world and founded another.

The future first archbishop of Mexico was a long-limbed na-tive of Biscay. Someone should make a typology of the raging Counter-Reformers: all of them were gaunt and somewhat common-looking people, men who did their work with an ex-cessive zeal that surely no one demanded of them, who took seriously things that had been proposed and set down only for appearance's sake. Zumárraga may also have been the only in-corruptible Spanish subject with whom Charles V—always sur-rounded by yes-men—ever managed to speak.

When Fray Julián Garcés, the first bishop of Mexico, retired at seventy-five—he was named to the seat so early that he established the diocese in Tlaxcala because Tenochtitlan still reeked of death—Zumárraga was named to the post. The emperor forced through his candidacy, popped a miter on his head, and shoved him off to America with the novel charge of "protector of Indians"—which he in fact was, so long as the Indians didn't display behavior suggestive of heresy.

Despite being a provincial man without political experience, Zumárraga had great instincts. He had hardly arrived in New Spain when he realized that the archdiocese had to be moved to Tenochtitlan—it wasn't yet clear at the time what the new kingdom's capital would be—and he settled it in the Convento de San Francisco at Mexico City, where the Torre Latinoamericana stands today.

On this spot, he moved into the cell of a common friar, bestowed on the Mexican Church the structure it has today, signed death sentence after death sentence with his bony hand, and realized that for the Christian faith to catch on, faces of saints and virgins would have to be painted brown and Catholic temples erected where Mexican places of worship had once stood.

Fray Juan didn't only have a thirst for fire. It was he who wrote the letter to the king of Spain describing the outrages of the Primera Audiencia government against the Indians, and it was he who came up with the plan of embedding the letter in a cake of wax and sending it hidden in a barrel of oil. With this wise and valiant act, he kept his promise of protecting the Indians—or at least the Indians he didn't think deserved to burn at the stake.

It's true that he burned all the indigenous codices that fell into his hands, considering them "things of the Devil." His fervor even took an investigative turn in matters of traditional medicine and the herbal arts: he did away with as many healers as he could, and silenced their apprentices. It was because of him that in a single generation the medical knowledge accumulated over thousands of years in central Mexico was lost. On the other hand, he had a passion for the books of learned men of the sort that he may have wished to be. When he left the Convento de San Francisco to move to the brand-new archdiocese built from the very stones of Tenochtitlan's Templo Mayor, he found the money to ensure that his primitive office and cell were jammed with books that he'd had sent from Spain: he was the founder of the first library in continental America. It was he who designed and shepherded the creation of the Universidad Pontificia de México, and he who bought and installed the first American printing press in the archdiocese.

All this happened once his battles were won and the lawyer Vasco de Quiroga was the unexpected bishop of Michoacán. Before this, when Quiroga and Zumárraga surely met at the office of the archdiocese in the Convento de San Francisco, both men (one of letters, the other aspiring to the name) were overwhelmed by a royal mandate that simply didn't seem feasible: transforming supine Mexico into something functional and resembling Europe. It was during one of these conversations that Zumárraga gave Quiroga the little book by Thomas More—evidence of this is the tome itself, which contains the notes of both men and can still be consulted in the rare books collection of the library at the University of Texas at Austin.

Exercitatio
linguae latinae

—◆•◆—

"In Paris do they play the way we play here?"

"With some variations: the Master of the Game gives the players shoes and caps."

"What are they like?"

"The shoes are made of felt."

"They would be of no use here."

"Here, of course, the game is played on streets strewn with stones; in France and Flanders they play on tile floors, flat and even."

"And what sort of balls do they play with?"

"Almost none are filled with air, as they are here; they are smaller than the balls you know, and harder, of white leather; they are stuffed with dog hair, not the hair of men done to death; and that is why the players hardly ever strike the ball with their palms."

"How do they play, then? With their fists, as we do with our balls?"

"No indeed, but with a racket."

"Strung with string?"

"With a thicker cord, like the strings of the *vi-huela*. They also stretch a line across the court: it's an error or fault to hit the ball beneath the line."

JUAN LUIS VIVES, *Practice of the Latin Language*, 1539

Third Set, Third Game

—•—

Drunks and children urinate with the same glorious urgency: when they have to go, they have to go with desperate seriousness. And they pee profusely and noisily, in a foamy, vast, and happy way.

15–love.

The poet felt a twinge of pleasure at the base of his skull at the liberation of his nether waters. His fuzzy head was bowed, because a last ray of light in his mind advised him to avoid splashing his boots. He raised his face and moaned like a lion, transfixed with delight. Only then did the stream regulate itself, allowing him to turn some of his attention to the dark figure of the Italian *capo*, who was spilling his own waters on the venerable cobblestones of the Via dell'Orso.

He felt as if he'd been pissing for hours when he finally pulled up his breeches and leaned against the wall to wait for his companion to finish. Only then did he notice that the cold air was poisoning him. He breathed deeply, straddling his legs to find solid footing. He clung—discreetly, he believed—to the ledge of the tavern wall so that the city would stop spinning.

The *capo* slouched at his side when he was done pissing. The poet saw him as if from a distance, his contours smeared by a brain turned to wax. His new friend seemed untouched, though they'd been drinking at the same pace. He also seemed to be talking interminably. The poet couldn't understand a word he was saying.

He made an effort to follow, feigning a probity he no longer possessed, and he gathered that the *capo* was saying something about the night and the river. He tried to stand up straighter and couldn't: he lost his balance and caught himself by throwing an arm around his companion's shoulders. The *capo* whispered in his ear what he had been saying all along without being understood. That they should go to the river, that the river cured all.

There's a particular kind of suffering in the loneliness of the person who has already lost the battle against alcohol and surrendered in a waking state: pain, nausea, the fear that this all-consuming discomfort will be eternal. At the river, he thought, he might be able to vomit without disturbing the neighbors with his retching. The warm hand of the Italian holding him up around the ribs was like the last hope in a world where all possibility of pleasure had suddenly been voided. He let himself be detached from the ledge, arm slung over the shoulders of the *capo*, who neither lost his composure nor stopped whispering things for his own entertainment as he guided the poet slowly along the narrow street. It wasn't healing that he'd found on the shoulder on which he was drooling. It was something at once less effective and more comforting.

15–15.

The boil of the river didn't have the healing effect he had

hoped for. Instead, the swampy dampness of the air made him feel even worse. He leaned on the stone balustrade, the city spinning in the hollows of his eyes, and breathed as deeply as he could. Since the situation wasn't improving, he shoved his index finger against the back of his throat. His whole body began to convulse, hunched over.

First it was just a pain in his chest, a surge of shivers and tremors, coughs so deep that he thought they would shake his balls loose. He crouched down, and felt the grappa that was still slopping unprocessed in his stomach surge up with cyclone force. He managed to rise enough to vomit interminably over the retaining wall of the waterway.

He wiped his mouth with his sleeve and blew his nose, which was running profusely, with his handkerchief. He rubbed his neck and slumped to the ground, resting against the balustrade. He smiled: no longer did he feel the graze of death's teeth on his scalp, but he was still very drunk. Only now did he seek the *capo* with his gaze. The Italian seemed to have vanished after leaving him at the river. He fell asleep.

30–15.

He was woken by someone shaking him by the shoulders. It was the *capo*, eyeing him with a complicit smile. Are you all right, he asked gently. He lifted the poet's face by the chin, gave him a few kindly slaps, pulled him by the ears. Stirred back to life, he saw that the man was offering him a jug. If I drink another drop of wine I'll die, he said. It's water, the *capo* said; fresh, I went to the fountain. This struck the poet as funny and he proceeded to rid himself of the sour taste of his own filth, spitting mouthfuls of water over the balustrade into the river.

Finally he splashed his face and neck. The Italian took a branch of mint from his bag. Chew this, he said. The poet obeyed with the humility of the fallen who are on their way back to life. Though the effect of the leaves on his palate and tongue was too intense to be pleasant, he felt that the mint juices were opening blocked ducts.

He grew confident enough to stand again. They're waiting for me at the Tavern of the Bear, he said to the *capo*, slurring his words. He took two steps, slipped, and fell like a side of beef. He was barely sober enough to catch himself with his hands and protect his head. As he tried to get up again, he saw the Italian doubled over with laughter. The very red face of the man who a moment ago had feigned commiseration struck him as hilarious. The *capo* came over, took him by the hand, and then the two of them ended up in the mud. Each tried to get up on his own, but whenever one of them had nearly managed it, the other brought him down again with his efforts. At last they declared defeat and lay on the ground together, belly up.

The street is too muddy, said the *capo*; we can't go back to the tavern like this. They crawled back to the balustrade. There are stairs here, said the Lombard, pointing to one of the flights down the retaining wall toward the stream; let's sit. They advanced clumsily until they found what they believed to be solid ground.

30–30.

They sat there next to each other, the edges of their knees knocking as they rocked with laughter at whatever was said. At some point the *capo* leaned back and rested his elbows on the step above, shook his head, and pulled a wineskin from his cloak. It's Spanish, he said to the poet. I can't believe you're going to keep drinking. The Italian uncorked the wineskin with a defiant look, crooning a silly little song. He raised it, opened his mouth, and let the stream of wine soak his mustache. Give me a swig, said the Spaniard, his boldness fueled by oblivion. The Italian let a second stream fall into his own mouth, full and still as a pool, and left his mouth open, pointing to indicate that it was the Spaniard's for the taking. The poet smiled before moving delicately to lap the wine with his tongue.

30–40. Break point, cried the duke.

He plunged his hand into the Lombard's hair and pressed against his mouth. The *capo*'s response was muscular: he grabbed the back of the Spaniard's head. The poet felt that he was returning to some long-lost place, a place where he had a guide. He followed as if on that tongue he might find something he had always lacked. The musky scent of the *capo*'s hair, the vigor of his embrace. The Lombard switched positions, rolling the poet underneath him and letting the full weight of his body fall on him. The Spaniard found an unexpected pleasure in yielding, as if the virtue of obedience had suddenly gained meaning. He felt the Lombard's erection growing. He was carried away by curiosity, the need to touch that wild and living thing that threatened and flattered him all at once. He was curious; he wanted to reach the place where everything that was happening would become happy torture. He touched the Lombard's cock. The *capo* pulled away from his mouth and began to run his tongue along his neck, his ears. He had to know; that was all he wanted: to know. He slid his hand under the Lombard's sash, buried it in his breeches and felt the *capo*'s member against his palm, squeezing it, exploring it, intrigued by its oils. He moved his hand a little lower to investigate the testicles, that source of pleasing heat. Then he heard the duke's unmistakable voice crying from the balustrade: What the fuck is going on here?

Cacce per il milanese.

Utopia

◆─•─◆

No one has ever read Thomas More's *De optimo reipublicae statu deque nova insula Utopia* in such a delirious state of pragmatic fervor as Vasco de Quiroga. It had been scarcely two years since the lawyer arrived in tumultuous New Spain, and he was already establishing the Indian hospital-town of Santa Fe outside Mexico City, whose ordinances—or what remains of them, which isn't much—can conclusively be counted as the foundational text of the long and lavish history of plagiarism in Mexico.

Thomas More had written a political essay disguised as a book of fantasy about how a society might work if stripped of the constitutive vice of greed. The volume was a sardonic meditation on the miseries of life in the England of Henry VIII: a political cartoon. Such a cartoon, in fact, that it described a place called Nolandia (or *"No hay tal lugar,"* according to the still-unmatched Spanish translation by Quevedo); a Nolandia that was bathed by the river Anydrus—"Nowater"—and whose ruler was known as Ademus, or "Peopleless." Utopia was an exercise, a Renaissance humanist game that was never intended to be put into practice. But Vasco de Quiroga saw something else in it.

New Spain and Nueva Galicia were places, but places that were more like no-man's-lands, because Hernán Cortés and Nuño de Guzmán had more experience kicking down what they found than putting the pieces back together. They were never statesmen, because they had come to Mexico to become millionaires. Most of the members of the conquistador generation started businesses; others, some of the best of them, built churches. Zumárraga built pyres and a library. Vasco de Quiroga judged it the natural thing to build a utopia.

In the hospital-town of Santa Fe, built around a home for the elderly and sick, the highest authority, Vasco de Quiroga, decreed that no money would circulate. As closely as it could within the bounds of reality, the town followed the non-instructions set forth by the London humanist for the functioning of Utopia: it was divided along two axes that intersected at the hospital and the church, and in each quadrant there were multifamily houses belonging to four different clans. These clans were administered by a council of elders, and each had its own representatives; they all reported to the director of the hospital, which was the only post that was required to be occupied by a Spaniard. To support itself, Santa Fe was founded with artisan families specializing in different practices: potters, carpenters, and featherworkers in one quadrant; bricklayers, pipe-fitters, and cacao merchants in another; and so on. All were organized into a system of masters and apprentices from the same family. The inhabitants of the village spent part of their time working in their specialty and another part sowing and harvesting on the village's communal land. Anything produced on the land or in the workshops that wasn't consumed locally was collected at the rectory, to be sent for sale in the markets of the capital.

Vasco de Quiroga must have thought that he was an economic genius and Thomas More a visionary, because Santa Fe was a dazzling success and soon became a production center supplying the capital not only with useful objects—tools, musical instruments, construction rods, and luxury goods such as polychrome statues of saints and virgins, or feather ornaments made according to the ancestral techniques of the Nahua featherworkers—but also with basic agricultural products: corn, squash, legumes, honey, flowers. It didn't occur to Quiroga, of course, that the model worked because the society that More proposed and he had orchestrated was a production system similar to the one that the Indians in the Valley of Mexico already had in place before the arrival of the Spaniards; it was the same scheme that the Indians had periodically tried to revive, for which Zumárraga would burn them at the stake.

In 1536, between burning indigenous books that today would be exceedingly valuable and printing treatises in Latin that are still available and that no one bothers to consult, Bishop Zumárraga pulled strings at the Spanish court to get the Vatican to recognize Mexico as a new region so that he could be promoted to Archbishop of New Spain. His maneuverings were successful—the king could deny him nothing—and in 1537 his conversation partner and lawyer friend, Vasco de Quiroga, was hurriedly ordained priest and became the first bishop of Mechuacán.

There, in the old Purépecha capital of Tzintzuntzan, Quiroga founded a second Indian hospital-town; and while he was at it, the next year he founded a full Indian utopian republic on the shores of Lake Pátzcuaro, in which each town specialized in the manufacture of some useful product and all the land was communal.

If there was a Wimbledon of dead humanists, Vasco de Quiroga would play in the final against Erasmus of Rotterdam and he would win by a landslide. Never was a man so comfortable in the role of designing a whole world to his own specifications. And if ever there was, no one did it so well. The utopian communities of Lake Pátzcuaro were the orchard of New Spain for three hundred years; the descendants of the Indians who founded them almost five hundred years ago still speak Purépecha, still govern themselves to a certain degree through councils of elders (I witnessed one in Santa Clara and another in Paracho), still live in enchantingly lovely towns protected by more or less untouched ecosystems, and still make the products that Tata Vasco thought would sell well enough to ensure the community's survival. I am not exaggerating. Yesterday, at my corner deli in New York City, I bought a couple of perfect avocados grown in the orchards of Mechuacán by the descendants of Quiroga's Indians. Two letters are all that have changed. Today we call the place Michoacán.

The letter from Pope Paul III inviting the bishop of Mechuacán to the meetings of the Council of Trent arrived in Pátzcuaro, so it was an Indian who brought it to Tzintzuntzan, where Quiroga was handling hospital business and trying to resolve a dispute between the families of local Purépecha cloth producers and Mexica featherworkers. Tata Vasco was in a meeting with Diego de Alvarado Huanitzin when the letter from the pope arrived.

On the Causes of Poverty Under the Reign of Henry VIII

And what say you of the shameless luxury all about this abject poverty? Serving-folk, craftsmen, and even the farmers themselves show excessive vanity in diet and in apparel. What say you of the brothels, the infamous houses, and those other dens of vice, the taverns and alehouses? And what of all the nefarious games in which money runs fast away, condemning initiates to poverty or highway robbery? Cards, dice, foot-ball, quoits. And worst of all: tennis. Banish from the land these noxious plagues.

THOMAS MORE, *Utopia*, 1516

Third Set,
Fourth Game

—◆—•—◆—

In his expansive moments, the Italian ruled the court; he was stronger and much more seasoned and resourceful, but he was also a volatile player. He was easily distracted, hampered by an excess of pride, and the nine years that he had on his opponent made his hangover infinitely more destructive than the poet's—the effect of hangovers is directly proportional to the age of the sufferer, and the increase in discomfort isn't linear, it's exponential.

Cowed as he was, morally shattered at having been caught out the night before, the Spaniard had been focusing on the match not as an outlet for hubris but as a way to redeem himself in the duke's eyes and recover his dignity. Victory would come off the court, but he had to win the match to gain it. He was confident that he could win, because it had been hard for the Lombard to beat him in the third game. He even swaggered a little, something he hadn't done since the start of the match. Put some real money on me now, won't you, he asked in a rather shrill voice, glancing toward the side of the gallery where his patron and the escorts were sitting.

Fortunately for him, there had been no witnesses except the

duke to the spectacle the night before. As soon as he had heard the duke's cry, he'd pulled his hand out of the Lombard's codpiece and pushed him off, escaping easily from his embrace. The *capo*, as drunk as or drunker than the Spaniards, hadn't understood what was happening until he saw the poet standing over him, challenging him with his sword—of steel, not flesh—unsheathed. To me, Duke, to me, shouted the poet like a man possessed; I'm being robbed. The *capo*, trapped, raised his hands with a wolfish smile. He lifted his face toward the nobleman and said in Italian: The only thing I was robbing this man of is his virginity, sir; he's the kind who likes to take it up the ass and it's no trouble to me to give satisfaction. The poet lunged, brandishing his sword. The Italian rolled down two flights of steps and leaped up in a flash, sword and dagger out. He was still smiling. The duke understood at once that his friend's well-bred flourishes would hardly be enough to beat someone who could extricate himself from an awkward situation with such grace and good humor. The poet feinted again and the *capo* shook him off without even raising his sword. Let it go, said the duke; this is a man of war, not some salon fencer. Without lowering the blade he was pointing at the Italian, the poet asked: And my honor? The *capo* looked up: Now it seems even sodomites have honor. The Spaniard made a third feint. He felt in his heels the shuddering blow with which it was parried. Drop your sword, ordered the nobleman.

I'll crush him, you'll see, I'm going to crush him, said the poet with his eyes on the duke. He was spinning the racket in circles, trying to relax his wrist. I don't doubt it, the duke replied, but stay focused.

The mathematician shed his idiot savant's mutism for a moment and got up from his seat. He reminded the spectators that the only thing in play from now on was the match. And with a glance at the Spanish linesman: Are we in agreement that any further bets will be placed only on the final result? The nobleman, without entirely understanding the rule but stung all the same, said: Of course. The mathematician shouted at the top of his lungs that the last round of betting was now open.

Barral hesitated slightly before putting the small fortune he had collected on the line: the coins his master had given him, the coins he had won, and the coins he had grudgingly volunteered. The poet turned to look at him, offended: It's in the bag, Otero. Bet your next month's salaries, cried the duke. What salaries? The duke gave them more money. What if we lose? I'll pay you double. Double the bet? Double the salary, idiot. Barral collected it all and returned to the line to set a second stack of coins on the Spaniard's side, coming face-to-face with Saint Matthew, who snarled at him.

The night before, the *capo* had made exactly the same face when the Spaniard lowered his sword at last. A catlike gesture, shaking his head a little and showing his teeth with mocking ferocity. The poet had backed up the stairs, the point of his sword keeping watch over his enemy. The Lombard made no move.

When the Spaniard reached street level, the grandee drew his own sword to wait at the ready for the Italian to come up. The *capo* rolled his eyes: What are you defending yourself for; you're no faggot like us. He put away his sword and dagger. Move aside, he said, and let me pass. It's all slander, the poet whispered to his patron. The *capo* offered his hand as he went by. When they ignored the gesture, he belched gloriously and paused to pull out his wineskin. His clumsy effort to uncork it told the Spaniards that he was still completely drunk. Now's our chance, said the duke, and they both fell on him. He shook them off, rolling on the ground. When they went after him again he had dagger and sword in hand and was waiting for them, smiling. Shall we settle this or not, said the *capo*; I'd rather go home now than spend the rest of the night with the bailiff, and you gentlemen are wanted in Spain. They lowered their swords. The duke sheathed his. We can't leave it like this, wailed the poet. You can't defend yourself in this state, said the duke; you don't know how to fight drunk. The Italian, his mind already elsewhere, was looking for his wineskin on the ground.

Discipline on the Roman side of the court seemed to have lapsed with the announcement of the closing of bets, because the painter was now drinking from a flask of wine that Mary Magdalene tipped voluptuously into his mouth. If he starts to drink too much, you'll have him where you want him once and for all, said the duke; keep playing as you have been. The Lombard had now turned and his tart was massaging his shoulders. The last spectators put down their bets. Don't you find it a little worrisome that absolutely no one else has put money on our side? said Barral.

The poet made a final attempt to redeem his honor at sword's point. The Italian toppled him, planting the tip of his own sword on the Spaniard's neck. Your friend will never learn, he said, with a glance at the duke. And addressing himself to the poet: Actually, why don't you turn over and I'll shove it up your

ass? He grabbed his balls. Just then they heard the nearly mo-
nastic little footsteps of the mathematician. What are you
doing? he called. Leave that boy alone and come home. The
Italian put his sword away again. Can I go to bed now? he asked,
fixing the poet with his gaze. He's a killer, the duke put in,
trying to make his friend see reason. The artist made a reverence: Thanks. The professor put an arm around him to lead
him away. Why does everything always have to end like this, he
said, and addressing the Spaniards: Please forgive him, gentlemen, he's drunk; tomorrow he won't remember a thing. Their
backs were turned when the poet howled: I challenge him to a
duel. They were all quiet for a second. The duke said: Shit,
fuck, and piss.

Let's do it now, yelled the poet with all he had. The artist—
his head resting on Mary Magdalene's bosom, his eyes closed—
tossed him the ball disdainfully, not even turning to look at
him. The poet caught it firmly in the air. I wager you can't guess
whose hair the ball in your hand is stuffed with, cried the artist,
still smiling. The Spaniard shrugged his shoulders. He genuinely didn't care. He bounced the ball on the ground and walked
to the line of service. The scapular, said the duke; touch the
scapular. The poet waited until the artist was settled on his side
of the court to yell *Tenez!*

The mathematician and the *capo* turned to stare at the poet.
Do you have any idea what you're saying, bugger boy, said the
capo; I'll kill you and then I'll be beheaded for it. The duke put
his hand to his forehead. Brother, he said; take back what you
said this instant, I beseech you. Well? asked the *capo*. At noon,
said the poet; in Piazza Navona; you choose the weapons. The

mathematician and the artist shook their heads in disbelief; the duke ran both hands through his hair, puffed out his cheeks, exhaled. What weapons, then? he asked. The professor cut in before his friend could answer. Rackets, he said; the weapons will be rackets and the duel will be in three sets, with betting; whoever takes two is the winner. The *capo* was shaking with laughter when, to the fury of the poet, the duke confirmed: Piazza Navona, noon, *pallacorda*. How do we know you'll be there? asked the poet, deflated. Everybody knows me, said the Italian; I'm Caravaggio. Francisco de Quevedo, replied the Spaniard, his eyes starting from his head. And who is this? he asked, jerking his nose at the professor. Galilei; I'm lodged at the Palazzo Madama. The nobleman introduced himself: Pedro Téllez Girón, Duke of Osuna.

The poet put all the force he could into the serve. The ball hit the roof of the gallery. The artist waited for the rebound. He took it, hitting a hair-raising drive that went straight into the dedans. *Cacce per il lombardo,* cried the professor; *due, equali.*

Encounter of
Civilizations

❖━━━●━━━❖

Hernán Cortés to one of his captains at a peaceful moment, serenaded by the clamor of insects in the altiplano night: When these savages play ball, it's the winner who loses his head. The soldier scratches his beard. Spawn of the Devil, they are, he says; they'll have to be taught that it's the loser whose head rolls.

The Emperor's
Mantle

——◆ · ◆——

Don Diego de Alvarado Huanitzin, Nahua of noble birth
and master featherworker, was at his shop in San José de
los Naturales—once a farm of exotic birds under the Emperor
Moctezuma—when he met Vasco de Quiroga. They were introduced by Fray Pedro de Gante, who managed what was left
of the *totocalli* (as such farms were called) after the brutal years
of the invasion.

The lawyer and the featherworker were soon on a comfortable footing, since both were of noble birth, both had been part
of imperial courts in their youth, both had remained—over the
twelve most confusing years that their two vast and ancient cultures had known in who knows how many centuries—in the
unusual situation of actually being free.

Vasco de Quiroga had no reason to return to Spain and was
greatly excited by the idea of building a society on rational prin-
ciples. The Indian had nowhere to go back to, but he had managed to find a relatively secure and comfortable spot for himself
after years of darkness, misery, and fear. His aristocratic rank
was respected and his work was so admired that most of the
pieces made in his shop were sent immediately to adorn palaces

and cathedrals in Spain, Germany, Flanders, and the duchy of Milan.

Unlike most Mexicans, Don Diego de Alvarado Huanitzin did know what this meant: he had been to Europe. He belonged to the select group of highborn artists who were received by the Holy Roman Emperor on Cortés's first trip back to Spain, and he knew very well that the new lords of Mexico might be eaters of sausage made from the blood of pigs, but they were also capable of rising far above their barbaric ways when it came to building palaces, painting canvases, cooking animals, or—and this impressed him most of all—making shoes.

From the moment that the ship he had been obliged to board (though not herded onto like cattle) sailed out of sight of American lands, Huanitzin realized that in order to survive his new circumstances he would have to learn Spanish. By the time they arrived in Seville, after stops in Cuba and the Canary Islands, he was attempting polite phrases in the language of the conquistadors and was able to say that he and his son would be happy to make a heavy cloak of white feathers for His Majesty: the sailors had told him that Spain was known for being cold.

Cortés loved the idea of the featherworker and his son making a small demonstration of their art in court—he himself had a spectacular feather mantle on his bed at his house in Coyoacán showing the birth of water in springs and its death as rain—and he immediately gave Huanitzin favored status among his entourage. Not only did the featherworker speak Spanish—terrible Spanish, but he could make himself understood—he was the only one who seemed to show any interest in taking stock of his new circumstances.

Once in Toledo, the conquistador arranged for a workshop to be set up next to the palace stables and negotiated unrestricted access to the kitchen, where the preparation of ducks, geese, and hens afforded Huanitzin a sufficient supply of feathers to make a cape for an emperor who, the featherworker was beginning to understand, had defeated the Aztec emperor because he was infinitely more powerful, even though he lived in a dark, drab, and icy city.

After setting him up in his new shop and providing him with satin, glue, paints, brushes, tools, and the assistance of the royal cooks, Cortés asked Huanitzin what else he needed in order to pay tribute to the emperor. Shoes, he replied. What kind, asked the conquistador, imagining that he must be cold and want woolen slippers. Like yours, said Huanitzin—who, being an Aztec noble and a featherworker, considered a provincial squire turned soldier to be of a class beneath his. With cockles. Cockles? asked Cortés. The Indian pointed to the captain's instep, festooned with a golden buckle and inlaid with mother-of-pearl. Buckles, said the conquistador; shoes with buckles. That's it.

Naturally, Cortés didn't buy Huanitzin a pair of shoes stitched with silver thread like his—not only were they monstrously expensive, walking in them was like squeezing one's toes into a pair of flatirons—but he did buy him good high-heeled boots with tin buckles, and along with them a pair of stockings, a few white shirts, and a pair of black breeches intended for some nobleman's son that fit the featherworker like a dream.

The Indian accepted the garments as if they were his due—without paying them much attention or thanking him for them—and made one last request of the conquistador before getting to work: Could you also find me some mushrooms? Mushrooms? To see mellifluous things while I'm worrying the king's drape. It's called a royal cape, a *capón real*. I thought that a capon was a bird with its burls cut off. Balls. Not balls, it's mushrooms I want. Here they would burn us both if they discovered you drunk on mushrooms. I'd hardly be dunked in them, it's not as if they're a pond. There are none in Spain. Well then, the royal *capón* won't be as mellifluous.

Huanitzin liked his new clothes, though he didn't think them fitting for a master featherworker who was once again on the grounds of an emperor's palace, so he used his first Spanish goose feathers to embroider one of the shirts—the one he wore on special occasions—with pineapples that he imagined were the equivalent of the Flanders lions he'd seen worked in gold on Charles V's cloak. The breeches were sewn down the side seams with bands of white feathers, turning him into a first wild glimpse of mariachi singers to come. The cooks spoiled this tiny man, who inspected their birds' scrawny necks and armpits in a getup like a saint on parade. When he decided that a fowl was worthy of being plucked, he kneeled over it, took a pair of tiny tweezers from his sash, blew the hair out of his eyes, and with maddening care defeathered the part of the bird that interested him—the cooks knew by now that once he chose a specimen it would have to be moved to the dinner menu because there was no way he'd be done with it before lunch. Hours later, he would return happily to his shop, generally with a harvest of feathers so modest that it hardly filled a soup plate. Sometimes he looked over the birds and found none to be of interest—there was no way to predict which he would judge worthy material for the king's cape. Other times it happened that there would be no birds cooked that day. When this was the case he still lingered in the kitchen, leaning on the wall so as not to be in the way. He admired the size of the chunks of animal moving on and off the hearth. What is that, he asked every so often. Calf's liver. He would return to his shop to tell his son that the king was to eat castle adder that night. But what is it? Must be a fat snake that lives in ruined towers, he explained in Nahuatl.

By the time the letter from Pope Paul reached the last outpost of Christianity, which just then was the Purépecha village half rising from the ruins of what had once been the imperial city of Tzintzuntzan, everyone was already calling Huanitzin "Don Diego," and he was still wearing the cotton shirts embroidered with pineapples that he believed were the height of European fashion, as well as his Toledo boots. By now he also read and spoke Latin, utterly garbled by his artilleryman's ear. Look, said Vasco de Quiroga, handing him the letter on which he had just broken the papal seal of Paul III. The featherworker read it, running his finger under the lines. I'll go with you, he said at last, so I can pay my regards to Charles.

Don Diego didn't miss the old gods. His mostly symbolic relationship with the succession of religious beliefs that life had visited upon him was based on rituals that felt just as empty when he offered up his work to the four Tezcatlipocas of the four corners of the earth as when he offered it to the three archangels and the Nazarene. Must we call him the Nazarene, asked Tata Vasco—who greatly enjoyed their conversations—every so often. That's what he was, Don Quiroga, a Nazarene, and you

know that I'd prefer you to call me Don Diego; I wasn't baptized just to be your latchkey. Lackey, Don Diego, lackey. He
liked it that the incense and blessings came only on Sundays
and lasted barely an hour—I'll be back in a splash, he would say
at the shop to announce that he was going to mass—and that
praying didn't involve piercing the member with a maguey
spine, and that the culmination of the Communion ceremony
was just a little piece of unleavened bread and not the corpse
stew eaten at the palace under Moctezuma—human flesh was a
little gummy and the dish in which it was served was over-
spiced. He didn't miss the blood spurting from the sacrificial
heart, the hurling of heads at crowds dazed on hallucinogens,
the rolling of decapitated bodies down steps.

He did miss the order and hygiene of the Aztec government;
the police who did their jobs, the sense of belonging to a tight
circle of friends who ruled a world that didn't stretch very far;
the security of knowing that he only had to speak Nahuatl to be
understood by everyone. And he was still grieving. No matter
how pleasant his situation, he would have preferred that the
Spanish invasion had never happened, that his parents had died
of old age and not of thirst during the siege; he would have
preferred that his wife hadn't been raped to death by the Tlaxcaltecas and that the Spaniards' dogs hadn't eaten his twin
daughters. He would have liked to bury his brothers and cous-
ins, killed in combat, and he would have preferred that his
brothers' wives hadn't been taken as slaves, hadn't had to choose
to throw their babies into the lake rather than see them endure
the life that awaited them.

Huanitzin had hidden in the *totocalli* with his eldest son

when the sack of Tenochtitlan began, and the two of them had been saved because Cortés had a weakness for the art of feather-work. With everything lost, Huanitzin had started over, and he felt that he had exchanged one set of privileges for another. His son would never wear the proud calmecac topknot, but he wouldn't go to war either; he wouldn't learn the poems that had made the empire great, nor would he enjoy the privilege of being considered an almost sacred artist at the palace, but he had gained the wonderful, liberating joy of horseback riding, and all the things new to Indians that he liked about this world: the shoes, the beef, the elegant shirts with pineapples that were by now the trademark of his house and that in the times of Mocte-zuma would have been considered an effrontery punishable by death.

No, said Vasco de Quiroga, I think I'll go alone; it's a meet-ing of bishops to save the Church, not the gypsy caravan Cortés brought along to entertain the king. The featherworker shrugged his shoulders: If you need anything, let me know. What could I possibly need? I don't know—a handsome peasant to take to the pope? A peasant? To flail him, as a sign of our devotion. No one touches His Holiness. Of course, that's why he's pope, but I'm sure his bishops flail him. Hail him. That's right, flail him. Not a handsome peasant, the padre continued to provoke him. Why? He's a man of God, Huanitzin; he must be eighty years old. It's a matter of coming up with the right peasant, Huanitzin con-cluded, wrinkling his brow and fingering the scanty beard he might better have shaved. How can you think of a peasant for the pope? A nice one, answered the Indian. Then, unperturbed, he bid the bishop goodbye: I'm off, it's raining now.

Though Huanitzin was part of the Tzintzuntzan hospital-town, he decided to build the aviary and his featherworking shop some distance away. Quiroga had decreed that his hospital be built on top of what was once the palace of the Purépecha emperor, and the Indian was of the opinion that it couldn't be a good place. I'm not going to build a *totocalli* on that crossload of souls, he'd said, it'll be the death of my little birds; and then we work at night, there's no knowing what we'll see when we have to clot ourselves with mushrooms so we can do mellifluous work. Quiroga accepted his reasoning; it was true that to calibrate the luminescent effect of the precious feathers, the artists worked mostly at night and in environments of controlled light: windowless sheds in which the only sources of light were beeswax tapers. I've already chosen the little plot where I'll build the shop, Huanitzin said to Quiroga; or better yet, why don't you come and deed me it, since you're a lawyer.

The plot was a sloping valley that began on a mountainside covered in the black fringe of a pine forest, and it ran down to the shores of a lake. It was completely isolated from the other settlements, the emerald meadow cropped by a flock of sheep, the mountains watchful in the distance. It was by far the most beautiful spot Quiroga had seen in the basin of Lake Pátzcuaro, which was itself, in his opinion—and mine—the most beautiful place in the world. Where are you going to put the shop, the bishop asked the featherworker. The Indian pointed to the top of the valley: Will you deed me the whole valley or just the shop? In Mechuacán there are no deeds, replied the padre; everything belongs to everyone. I ask because it belongs to some Purépecha, said Huanitzin, but they only want it to plant squash and keep sheep. The bishop thought for a moment: You can put the shop here, but only if you start a town of featherworkers. How will I flounder a town, when I have only one son? Bring in the Purépecha. Do you mean I should teach them featherwork? The bishop nodded. And you'll give me my deeds? Quiroga harrumphed and shook his head: I can give you a declaration of origination. And some deeds for my little shop. No.

For months, another Indian, who called himself a notary and said that he represented the interests of Don Diego de Alvarado Huanitzin and the newly founded village of Nearby, waited from sunup to sundown in the antechambers of the archdiocese without being received by Quiroga. Finally, the bishop made up some deeds just to get rid of him. Only then did he learn that in the perfect valley he had visited with the featherworker, a workshop had already been built, as had houses for five families and a communal dining hall.

Third Set, Fifth Game

———•———

The duke lost the composure that he'd been careful to maintain all through the match when he saw how the Lombard drilled the ball into the dedans. Motherfucker, he said. Barral whispered in his ear: We're in fine shape, boss. Neither of them had ever seen a drive like that, so fast it was almost invisible, so precise it was as if—instead of going into the hole—the ball had been swallowed up by the wall.

The duke asked for a time-out and beckoned to his protégé. The poet could still feel victory in his fingertips and he was convinced that his opponent's smash had been chance. We've been watching him try for it the whole match, he said to the duke, and this is the first time he's done it; it must have been luck. The duke shook his head. Barral raised a finger, requesting permission to have his say. What is it, asked his master. Or he's been stringing us along so that we'd bet the rest. A shadow of doubt crossed the poet's face. The man is crippled by his hangover, he said; I don't think he'd put himself through this just to win a few coins. Faugh, said the duke: For now, forget about backspin on your serve; aim for the end of the gallery so that he isn't so close to the dedans and he has to lob it.

The poet returned to his side of the court. *Tenez!* He served a slow ball with no backspin that floated like a balloon onto the far corner of the roof. He watched it go up and noted, from the moment it began its descent, that he'd put it just where he wanted it. It would bounce oddly, drop in an awkward spot, and the Italian would have to lunge for it, hopefully with his backhand.

The duke managed to cry, Cover the dedans, catching the gleam in the artist's eye as he waited. The artist retreated behind the baseline, smiling, and crossed his arm over his body, preparing for a backhand strike. The Spaniard ran back. When he saw the bullet coming at him he ducked his head. The ball went into the dedans. *Caccia automatica per il milanese,* said the mathematician. *Tre–due.*

On the Vestments
of the Utopians

—◆ • ◆—

All the people appear in the temple in white garments. The priests' vestments are parti-colored, more wonderful for their craft and form than for their materials. They are neither embroidered with gold thread nor set with precious stones, but are composed of the plumes of several birds, laid together with so much art and so neatly that they are greater in value than the richest cloth. In the ordering and placing of these plumes some dark mysteries are represented.

THOMAS MORE, *Utopia*, 1516

The Pope's Peasant

—— • ——

Huanitzin's mountainside establishment was devoted exclusively to the art of featherwork, though sheep were tolerated because they cropped the grass, driving away the snakes and field rats. Anyone who chose to persist in fishing or planting squash was invited to leave by Don Diego's apprentices during terrifying nighttime visits with sticks and stones.

The settlement, because of its proximity to Tzintzuntzan and its tininess, never had a name, or had one only in the minds of Huanitzin and Tata Vasco, even though it was formally baptized as Cercanías, or "Nearby," in the sham deeds granted by the bishop, in honor of the stagecoach that ran between Toledo's main square, Talavera de la Reina, and Aranjuez when the featherworker was a visitor at the royal court: Huanitzin thought that Nearby was a place.

Of all the communities that made up the diocese, which was in reality Vasco de Quiroga's personal fiefdom, the bishop's favorite was Tupátaro, because it lay among the richest fields of New Spain; like all dictators for life, he was by nature better equipped to understand productive units than artist communities. Even so, when afternoons spent visiting the Tzintzuntzan hospital grew long, he would make a detour to Nearby to while away the time: the sun spilling behind the blue mountains, the lethal minute when the water of the lake lay still to let the souls of the dead pass, the emerald slide of the sheep-sheared meadow, the sudden arrival of the children. If he could have, he would have established the archdiocese in Tupátaro, instead of Pátzcuaro, so he could live there, but he couldn't help thinking that if he continued to be good, when he died he would go to Nearby.

From a distance, Quiroga noted that the houses, once built of sticks and palm fronds, were now adobe, and that the workshop was already an imposing structure, whitewashed and with a tile roof, and that the *totocalli* was perfectly organized. He moved on to greet the women, who were hard at work in the communal kitchen. Are the men in the shop? he asked. One of the women, who didn't speak Castilian but did speak Nahuatl, answered that for eleven days Diego had kept the men working behind closed doors, and wouldn't let the women see them even when they brought food. If things go on like this, continued another in Castilian, the children will run wild. But what are they doing? asked Quiroga. You know Don Diego and his mysteries, said one of the Purépecha in Castilian; he's still a Mexica through and through. The Nahuas are cryptic folk, concluded the bishop. Exactly right, answered the Indian woman; always crippling things. The priest thought to himself that in addition to the featherworking shop, Huanitzin had established another workshop, of imaginary Spanish.

The ladies set him a place at the table: Go on, Tata, eat something before the children come back. He couldn't resist a perhaps overly large helping of Mechuacán tamales even though that night he had to dine with Zumárraga's envoys, who would be coming late to the hospital to discuss the positions that the bishops of New Spain should take at Trent.

The situation was complicated: Charles V was in favor of including the dissident bishops of Germany and England in the sessions—the former because they were his subjects and the latter because Henry VIII was his great friend and he couldn't countenance not playing tennis with him again. In this regard, the presence of the novo-Hispanic bishops was essential, and especially that of Vasco de Quiroga: he had built a successful community on the very fringes of empire based on the ideas of a British humanist who also happened to be Henry VIII's laureled adviser. No one knew yet in New Spain that the English king had already ordered More's beheading and that this made Charles's position at Trent absolutely untenable: Rome now had the first martyr of what would soon be the Counter-Reformation, and it canonized him so fast that the novo-Hispanic bishops, like the Spaniards, never made it to Trent in the end.

But all this is what we know, we who live in a world in which past and present are simultaneous because history is written to make us believe that A leads to B and therefore progresses logically. A world without gods is a world in history, and in stories like this one: history and stories alike offer the consolation of order. Back then, the world—the world that Quiroga had invented—was a dizzying and directionless one, growing in the palm of one acknowledged God and other clandestine gods, all battling one another for the meaning of things; the basin of Lake Pátzcuaro was a drop of divine saliva in which, as in a dream, all mysteries were revealed.

He finished his last *tamal* and went to the door to watch the sun set behind the water and the hills. The children were on their way back from the lake; children who spoke a mix of Purépecha, Nahuatl, and Castilian; children of Quiroga whom Quiroga believed to be children of God. He thanked the ladies and went walking along the emerald bank of the hill, slapping the mosquitoes on his neck. At the end of the path, the wild light of the candles that Huanitzin required for his work swelled along the bottom of the barred door.

The bishop had no memory of a recent featherwork commission. Not one so big that it would require the artist to shut himself away for eleven days with all his apprentices. He clapped a few times to scatter the sheep that had already settled with their young on the path, and to let the featherworkers know that he was coming. He caught his breath, and knocked at the door. He cried: It's me, Don Diego; Tata Vasco. The featherworker opened the door to him with the dazed look and clenched jaw of those who aren't entirely with us; he had obviously been working without pause for eleven days as the ladies had claimed, sleeping as little as possible and scarcely eating. Can I come in, asked the bishop. Huanitzin—the creases under his eyes reddened—smiled with a pride that the priest always found a little frightening, as if a sudden awareness of his artist's mastery could abruptly turn into action and erase in a single sweep the passage from these lands of the Christian God, who might in the end not be needed after all. Come in, he said, blowing at his hair with a half smile; all the candles lighting the workshop flickered.

Inside, laid out on the table, blazed the most astonishingly delicate and powerful group of luminescent pieces the bishop had seen in his life. What are they? he asked the Indian. The peasant for the pope. A peasant is a common campesino, said the bishop, a bit exasperated at being suddenly returned to the vulgarity of language and politics. The Indian shrugged: If you want we'll get him an Otomi, but I think this peasant is nicer.

The bishop came up and took one of the pieces in his hands. Careful, the glue isn't dry yet, said the Indian. Are they miters? Easter miters, explained the featherworker, for His Holidays to wear during Holy Week, a reminder that we are his warriors. Holiness, said the bishop, though his intention wasn't to correct the featherworker's Spanish, but to point out that if ever a human entity could be described with such an adjective, this was it. What a load we have to bear, Huanitzin, he said; you're the man of God. The mushrooms help, even if you don't like them; will you have some? There are a few left, I think. Are they *derrumbes* or *pajaritos*? *Derrumbes* and also *pajaritos*. A little handful of *pajaritos*, then, but that's all, I have a meeting soon.

They went out to watch the fading of the last light of day. They were silent until Quiroga noticed that the meadow had begun to breathe and the surface of the lake had become a window onto the world of the old gods. They were playing ball, indifferent to their extinction. Aren't the light-sheep mellifluous, Huanitzin said to the bishop, giving him a nudge to shake him from his stupor. The trees, my dear Don Diego, the trees; how lovely to see them grow fat with sap. Now you are truly ready to appreciate His Holidays' miters, said the Indian, seized with laughter.

Arte de la lengua
de Mechuacán

◆—•—◆

GAME PLAYED WITH ROSES AS IF WITH BALLS—
Tsitsiqui apantzequa chanaqua

GAME PLAYED BY TOSSING TWO OR THREE
BALLS UP IN THE AIR AND CATCHING THEM—
Tziman notero tanimu apantzen mayocxquareni

BALL GAME PLAYED WITH THE HANDS—
Apantzrqua chanaqua

BALL GAME PLAYED WITH THE KNEES—
Taranduqua hurincxtaqua

BALL GAME PLAYED WITH THE BUTTOCKS—
Taranduqua chanaqua

FRAY MATURINO GILBERTI,
Art of the Language of Mechuacán, 1558

Third Set,
Sixth Game

Your only chance, then, is to get the serve to bounce on the roof's edge, said the duke; they've been toying with us, but he might still slip up, and on the return you kill him. The poet bit his lower lip without saying anything, then shook his head: Thoughts, Otero? The escort shrugged his shoulders: Block the dedans with your body. That's obstruction, noted the poet. It's street rules: if the ball is heading straight for the dedans, you can stop it however you like and the game is yours. The poet raised his eyebrows. Mine? Only madmen play the dedans. If I obstruct that ball it'll break my arm. Block it with your back. The dedans is too high for that. Exasperated, the duke said: Just win, no matter how you do it.

Tenez! He got the serve right: strong and at the corner. Impossibly, the artist reached it and hit another drive that was clearly going into the dedans. Hopeless and out of options, the poet blocked it. Or rather, his forehead did.

As he lost consciousness, he heard a murmur of appreciation rising even from the Italian side of the stands. He also heard the relentless mathematician's voice: *Tre a tre.*

The duke turned his head to Barral, still unsure about the call. He's right, the soldier confirmed: street rules. So now it's sudden death, said the nobleman, in genuine admiration of his protégé's courage. If your poet isn't dead already, added the mercenary.

Seven Miters

——— • ———

Descriptions of works of art, like descriptions of dreams, halt stories and sap their strength. A work of art can be part of the story only if it alters the line of history as it's being drawn, and yet if a work of art, like a dream, is worth remembering, it's precisely because it represents a blind spot for history. Art and dreams don't stick with us because they have the capacity to move things along, but because they stop the world: they function as a parenthesis, a dyke, a moment of rest.

It might be worth taking a trip with seven stops to see the seven miters from the workshop of Don Diego Huanitzin in the museums where they're on display. One is in Toledo Cathedral, another in Vienna's Museum of Ethnology, another in El Escorial, another at Florence's Silver Museum, and another—the one that Caravaggio saw—in the Veneranda Fabbrica del Duomo di Milano. The most battered are those at the Musée des Tissus in Lyon, France, and the Hispanic Society of America in New York. They are seven incredible, tall caps, decorated with scenes from the Crucifixion macerated in the mushroom-glutted brains of a group of Indians from Michoacán. One features the family tree of Saint Joseph, but on each of the other six is an emblem formed by the monograms *IHS* and *MA*, graphic representations of Jesus and Mary. The central space of each piece is occupied by the *M*, on which Christ is crucified as if on a tree, over which his limbs drape.

The miter that Paul III handed down to Pope Pius IV and that Pius IV then presented to San Carlo Borromeo at the loggia of the Colonnas—the very one that Federico, the saint's cousin, brought with him to Rome for the Lenten masses he was to hold immediately after he took refuge at the Palazzo Giustiniani—is probably the best preserved of the seven. In addition to the traditional Easter motifs—the pillar, the steps, the lance, the Calvary, the crown of thorns—Carlo Borromeo's miter is decorated with motifs that the saint must have imagined hailed from some other world, because they did. Birds, trees, clouds, near-angelic flying creatures, rays that at once weave and cradle the classic Catholic figures, presenting them as what they were in the Mexico of the time: politely accepted but superficial impositions; little bodies set in a neurological system that saw the story of the world in its own way, a world complete with its own viewing instructions. The son rising up on the monogram of the mother not as tortured flesh in human history but as a bird that soars sunward after dying in combat. Flowers, seeds, and feathered creatures not as decoration but as the syllables of a universe in which the earthly and the divine are separated by nothing but the diaphanous veil of a collapsible consciousness. Angels scattering stars like seed.

On Carlo Borromeo's miter, the world is full of everything in the world, and its colors have an intensity simply unimaginable to the European eye of the time. One has to picture Caravaggio admiring its fine craftsmanship when he came to work at the cardinal of Milan's *studiolo* in Rome, discovering with surprise that the images weren't painted on cloth, as he'd thought at first, but were made of another material, organic and palpable, that changed in shade with the touch of a finger: a ray of light the tiny pathway along which the feathers had been stroked.

Vasco de Quiroga had already seen many pieces of feather-work art when Don Diego showed him the miters, but all the pieces he had seen before had been designed by friars; the Indians simply gave them color. In the workshop this time, the miters lit only by candlelight and splayed open on account of the mushrooms, Quiroga saw them as seven living flames, an outpouring of light undulating with the breath of the gods who, silent and indifferent, continued—still continue, perhaps—to weave the threads of the tapestry that cradles us.

By four in the afternoon, when the Roman sun came straight in the window, Caravaggio must have thought it was time to give up his work on the wall of Federico Borromeo's *studiolo* in his fruit basket painting. He must have stepped back a little to get a better look at his day's labor as he rolled his brushes in a cloth. Then he must have wiped his fingers on his trousers. Next, hypersensitive as he was to the refractions of light that he chased tirelessly back in his dark, closed studio, he must have noticed that the miter was changing color all by itself, as if it were alive.

With eyes like saucers from the effect of the mushrooms, Vasco de Quiroga cast his gaze over the surface of the seven miters. He felt the caress of the feathers on his eyelashes and he could see how the world they portrayed came to life like a hive in which everything was present and everything moved along a given path. The birds flew silently, the angels eternally scattered star-seed, the son rose up on the thrust of Earth's sacred vagina. He chose the miter that Caravaggio later saw, picked it up, and said: This one I'll present to Pope Paul myself.

Caravaggio raised his hands and took the miter from the shelf on which it sat. The gold of the pentagram with the letters *IHSMA* burst on his pupils, the figures attired in the blue of saints dragging his eyes in all directions, showing him how to see in a bigger way. He shook his head, as if to wrench himself from a dream. He moved the miter to a spot where the light fell directly on it and suddenly the whole thing was ablaze. The red, he thought, intent on unpicking the mystery of fire that doesn't burn, iridescence that doesn't blind. The red, said Vasco de Quiroga to Huanitzin; the colored figures are what move in God's sight, but the red framework beneath is God himself, his instructions. That's right, said the featherworker.

The poet opened his eyes. Everything was red. He touched his eyebrow where the ball had struck him. It was cut open. He felt a flurry of people around him. He raised his open hand to signal that he was all right.

Caravaggio tilted the miter, saw that the figures came to life. Their faces changed; Christ rose up in an exercise of celestial swimming that was his salvation and no one else's, the salvation of those who die in combat, no matter what kind—this novel is the combat. He half closed his eyes, which was the only way he could bring into focus the background of red leaves and branches that twined around the rest of the images. Whoever made this, he thought, can read God's design. When silence fell, the poet said: I'm still in. He had understood that this wasn't a game of tennis, but a sacrifice. The Indian smiled, showing what looked to the priest like the teeth of a warrior. The red is the blood of the earth, the veins of the world, said the bishop; God's design. The mushrooms help, said Don Diego. He continued: Take one with you for Don Zumárraga, so that he'll send you to see His Holidays; it's you who can best speak for us. The poet rose and picked up the ball and racket, the little figures retreating respectfully from the court that was swimming in a sea of red. It wasn't a game. Someone had to die at the end and it would be the young man he had been that morning; reborn would be the recalcitrant Catholic, the anti-Semite, the homophobe, the Spanish nationalist, the dark side of his two selves. He rubbed the scapular. Everything red. Caravaggio fell into Federico Borromeo's desk chair. Tracing the branches of the miter's red background, he felt that he could hear the plea of an ancient soul, a soul from a dead world, the soul of all those who've been fucked by the pettiness and stupidity of those who believe that winning is all that matters, the soul of those who've been undeservedly obliterated, the lost names, the dust of bones—his own bones on a Tuscan beach, Huanitzin's bones by Lake Pátzcuaro—the soul of the Nahuas and the Purépecha, but also of the Langobards, who a thousand years ago had been destroyed by Rome as Rome had just destroyed the Mexicas and would destroy the poet. He heard: It's you who can best speak for us. *Tenez!*

Sudden Death

—•—

Zoom. Dedans. *Caravaggio trionfa di nuovo a Roma.*

BIBLIOGRAPHIC NOTE

Like all books, *Sudden Death* comes mostly from other books. References to almost all of them appear in the novel itself, as the form allows. But there are two recent biographies of Michelangelo Merisi without which I couldn't have written the book: Andrew Graham-Dixon's *Caravaggio: A Life Sacred and Profane* and Peter Robb's *M: The Man Who Became Caravaggio*. Andrew Graham-Dixon established the relationship—now so obvious—between Caravaggio's paintings of beheadings and his Rome death sentence. Peter Robb traced the link between the mindsets of Galileo Galilei and Merisi as two poles of a single system. The research and investigation of both biographers into the role of Fillide Melandroni in the work of the artist are also at the heart of my book. Equally indispensable were Heiner Gillmeister's *Tennis: A Cultural History* and Cees de Bondt's *Royal Tennis in Renaissance Italy*. Alessandra Russo's work on material culture in the century of the conquistadors, especially as curator of the exhibition *El vuelo de las imágenes: Arte plumario en México y Europa*, at the Museo Nacional de Arte in Mexico City, sparked a good part of the writing of this story. The little that is truly historical in the novel comes from her work and from *Gusto for Things: A History of Objects in Seventeenth-Century Rome* by Renata Ago.

ACKNOWLEDGMENTS

This book was written with the support of the Dorothy and Lewis B. Cullman Center for Scholars and Writers at the New York Public Library and the Princeton Program in Latin American Studies. It was finished on a writer's residency as part of the program Castello in Movimento at Malaspina Castle in Fosdinovo, Italy.